Dempsey's Lodge

Dempsey's Lodge

Eric Wright

QUATTRO BOOKS

The publication of *Dempsey's Lodge* has been generously supported by the Canada Council for the Arts and the Ontario Arts Council.

 Canada Council Conseil des Arts
for the Arts du Canada

 ONTARIO ARTS COUNCIL
CONSEIL DES ARTS DE L'ONTARIO
50 YEARS OF ONTARIO GOVERNMENT SUPPORT OF THE ARTS
50 ANS DE SOUTIEN DU GOUVERNEMENT DE L'ONTARIO AUX ARTS

Cover design: Sarah Beaudin
Editor: Luciano Iacobelli
Typography: Grey Wolf Typography

Library and Archives Canada Cataloguing in Publication

Wright, Eric, author
    Dempsey's Lodge / Eric Wright.

ISBN 978-1-927443-48-4 (pbk.)

    I. Title.

PS8595.R58D44 2013   C813'.54   C2013-904293-8

Published by Quattro Books Inc.
Toronto ON

info@quattrobooks.ca MAR 1 2 2014
www.quattrobooks.ca

Printed in Canada

ON THE DAY OF the picnic, the pontoon that would carry most of the lodge's guests to the picnic island was waiting, tied to the big dock. The pontoon had been bought second hand or even third hand from a lodge a hundred kilometres away, then trucked across country and refloated at the town dock to begin a third (or fourth) life at Dempsey's, making one trip a week to the picnic island.

Brendan Copps stood on the veranda of the lodge, watching the guests assemble on the dock. Copps had not signed up for the picnic, wanting to spend a day by himself. The easiest way to do that, requiring the fewest explanations, was to ask for a guide to show him the country, to be a tourist. Copps was a policeman, a sergeant in the Ontario Provincial Police, a job that made strangers curious and made it difficult to be anonymous. He had dressed himself in a flat brown cap—designed in Britain, made in China, and bought in Minneapolis by Winnie while on a shopping expedition for herself—a blue striped T-shirt, bought in Croatia, and jeans, but it hadn't been a successful disguise. Usually he protected himself by adopting a profession dull enough to excite no interest. "I work for the government," he would say, "In Records." This time, though, he had been careless enough to let his real office know where he was going, and found a tiny message waiting for him when he checked in to the lodge, a message addressed to Sergeant Copps, O.P.P., something to do with an adjustment in the duty roster. It wasn't difficult to know that word had got around quickly. No one asked him casually what he did for a living.

Copps was forty and he had come to Dempsey's with the feeling that it was more than just another outing, that there was, appearing only in tiny fragments attached to other more ordinary thoughts, a hidden agenda. He felt a need to examine what seemed to him an entirely new urge to settle down. Thus he had come to the lodge for a week to see what would happen. He planned to play a little golf, not because golf was important or because he missed it but just to see if he ought to take it up again. He was at Dempsey's, he thought, to mark a passage, as if—no doubt about it—as if he was having a private stag party before he let that part of his life go. Goodbye to all that? Perhaps. At least, a week at Dempsey's seemed like a good idea, a good pause to think about the future.

From where he stood on the wooden deck that surrounded the upper floor of the lodge, Copps could watch the camp workers getting ready for the day. Two workers put cushions in a couple of small aluminum boats, lining them up on the other side of the dock to the big pontoon. Many of the guests who had finished breakfast were on the beach, waiting for the signal to begin boarding. Winnie, Brendan Copps's girlfriend, was talking to a pair of bird-watchers from Norfolk in England. This couple had come to Canada primarily to visit the bird sanctuary at Long Point in Lake Erie and had found the time to come to Dempsey's Lodge in the hope of seeing birds that they didn't see in Norfolk. They had made pleasant dinner companions, being curious about Brendan Copps and his job but very polite with their questions, and about what it was like to be Winnie, his girlfriend, a veterinarian specializing in large animals in a small town in Ontario. Paul Donner this bird-watcher's name was, married to Catherine—Kate, please—who had no interest in birds but was obviously happy to be married to a "birder."

"We go to interesting places," she said. "Paul looks at birds and I look at everything else, and at the end of the day we tell each other what we've missed."

Donner had a mildly ecclesiastical air that would have suited the role of the principal of a college founded by a church organization, a fringe of silver hair around a bald dome and a pink-and-white complexion that always looked freshly washed, thus creating the clichéd stage portrait of elderly innocence, wearing a blue linen blazer. Their dinner table the night before was completed by a little old lady from Brandon, Manitoba, and another middle-aged woman who was on her own, a Mrs. Hepburn, from Ottawa, who arrived at her seat talking and did not stop talking for fifteen minutes.

Copps very quickly realized that Mrs. Hepburn was no ordinary irritant and stopped even thinking about wresting the conversation away from her. He saw that the others were equally bemused, that everyone had decided to savour this phenomenon tonight as they resolved to get another table tomorrow. It was like being on a cruise ship.

Up to a point, that is. That point came while they were waiting, after soup, for the main course to arrive and Mrs. Hepburn was well into a monologue on families and babies, and came to a sub-topic of the desirability and difficulty of having twins. No one had done more than nod or grunt in the tiny gaps of her discourse, all busy with thoughts they would deal with later. Copps, at the moment, was replacing his early irritation with a private guessing game, wondering what was in the other diners' heads and guessing that, like him, they were constructing private meditations while using Mrs. Hepburn's chatter as a kind of white noise.

Up to a point. There came the moment in Mrs. Hepburn's monologue when she had finished listing twins she had known and was ready to move on to other multiple births. She paused to draw breath. Paul Donner had been smiling benignly with the look of someone who has arranged his face as he searched for a pleasantry to paper over the situation, but when Mrs. Hepburn seemed to be ready to list the advantages of quintuplets, Donner said, "It must save a lot of fucking," and looked around the table for agreement.

It was as if the bishop had farted. Copps looked up at the speaker, anticipating that Donner would be winking at the other diners, looking for complicity, but Donner looked through Copps' glance, and Copps saw that Paul Donner was a more complicated man than he had thought.

Mrs. Donner said, "Paul just came back from British Columbia where he was staying at a lumber camp looking for Arctic swans or some such and it's still affecting his vocabulary." She smiled, seeming in no way put out herself. Her husband stayed silent, bland-faced and sparkling.

Winnie said, "I thought the fish chowder yesterday was delicious, didn't you? I love chowder—I think it's worth driving to the Maritimes for—I've made a good chowder with canned clams but I've never tried it with freshwater fish…"

Mrs. Hepburn stood up and gathered together her shawl by handfuls as if collecting together the pieces that Paul Donner's remark had shattered. To Mrs. Donner she said, "You have to put up with language like that. I don't," and went away to the other side of the room where she found a seat at a table full of children.

Winnie started to protest her going, rising, putting out a hand. Copps reached out a leg and pressed Winnie's foot to keep her in place, then, in some sympathy with Winnie's instinct of kindness, recognizing that behind Mrs. Hepburn's drone there was probably some misery, he said, to Donner, "That was kind of an offensive use of language in strange company, wasn't it?"

"Of course it was. But what were *you* going to do?"

"Me? Nothing."

"Sit there listening to her through the coffee and the petit fours? Ask the manager if he could find you and your good lady another table tomorrow, perhaps, and create a problem for him, for us and even for the poor woman?"

"Or just put up with it."

"For how long? Three times a day for a week?" Donner shook his head. "I think my idea was better. Now, you see, no one's feelings are hurt, just Mrs. Hepburn's sensibility. Not her feelings, you understand: she won't take it personally, unlike almost anything else one might have done or said. I will get a reputation for uncouthness, not a high price for the pleasure of being able to talk to you two over dinner tomorrow, and the next day if you're staying." He waited while they thought this through.

"That's very clever of you," Winnie said, eventually.

"Yes it is, isn't it? Once I realized that if the woman was the victim of her tongue, then she was to be pitied and a way had to be found of separating her from us with her dignity, or pride, intact. No need to be rude, I thought, just vulgar. The woman, I would guess, is terribly lonely and fills the silence in the only way she can. She deserves your commiseration."

Mrs. Donner said, "Paul, let's show it by changing the subject. You're looking smug." She turned to Winnie. "Are you two going on the picnic tomorrow?"

Brendan Copps said he was going for a boat ride, Winnie thought she might go on the picnic, and the little woman from Brandon said she was for the picnic, too.

The Donners were going off on their own to look for birds.

Two other guests appeared; they were already known as "the honeymoon couple" because of their absorption in each other and because Mrs. Hepburn had asked them if that's what they were.

"You on your honeymoon?" she had asked, and the bride had made a face and turned away, indicating that she thought the question none of Mrs. Hepburn's business, but it was enough and soon the whole lodge knew. This couple was among the last to appear on the day of the picnic, eating breakfast at a separate table for two.

Eric Wright

Now Copps watched them walk along the beach to a canoe that had been made available for them. They seemed to be debating who should sit where and Copps wondered if they knew anything about canoeing. He relaxed when he saw that she was obviously insisting that he put on a life jacket.

Copps watched them load the canoe and climb in, she first, awkwardly, climbing down into the front, the canoe held steady by her husband. She held the canoe close to the dock, and he slid just as awkwardly onto the back seat. After a discussion, which Copps guessed was about which side each should paddle from, they set off, looking from a distance like an advertisement promoting Canada, her mane of shining black hair seemingly chosen to contrast with the blond helmet of her husband.

The last fishing boat was claimed by two old men who had sat at their own table the night before. They surprised Copps by carrying no tackle: no rods, no tackle box, no landing nets. Their guide was waiting for them on the shore and he, too, surprised the watching Copps by looking about as old as the guests, although, Copps thought, it's hard to tell with Natives.

Lenny Kollberg, the manager, said in Copps' ear, "They asked for the oldest guide, because they wanted to hear about the history of the area. That would have been Bert Tyrell, but you've got him and he didn't want to switch. When I told him about you he liked the idea of working for a copper, he said. The one I gave them, old Matthew, isn't really working any more but he said he would take them out as long as there was no shore lunch to cook, so we've made them a packed lunch and they've got a few beers. They used to be guides themselves somewhere around Kenora, when they were students. They're professors now, or they were, I guess, before they retired. You know, we're having a real pensioners' day out. Wayne Lucas and Mel Gladstone their names are, Mel is the short one with

14

not too much hair left. If you find yourself talking to them and forget their names, just call them 'Professor'. They won't mind."

"They used to be guides here?"

"Not here, no, at one of the camps up river that have closed up. As I say, they were students then, working for the summer..." A movement below caught his eye. "Excuse me; I have to check up on something." He left the veranda, hurrying down the stairs to the path around the lodge.

As the crowd of picnickers drained off the dock and onto the pontoon, Copps walked down to see Winnie safely on board. When she saw the excursion crowd loading on to the boat, two children already crying, a look of doubt had appeared on Winnie's face, and Copps urged her quickly along the gangplank. He was now looking forward to his day out and he did not want to give it up to walk twice round the little golf course with Winnie, nor did he want to take her with him. Winnie was for later and earlier, but not now. Once he found her a place on the boat where she could sit and read, acknowledging the scenery as it went by, the danger that she would balk and stay with him was past.

"Put some cream on your nose," she said. "And go fish or whatever you plan to do. And put a hat on."

He stood on the dock to wave goodbye in case she was watching, and then climbed back up to the balcony of the lodge to wave again. Finally, Mike Loon tooted the old steam whistle (now battery-operated) to warn latecomers, waited two or three minutes, then, when no one else appeared running, cast off and steered out into the lake. The two small boats followed in the wake of the pontoon and the guests cheered and called back and forth. It had been a hot, sunny week, and the older men and women were pleased to spend an hour under the boat's awning for a change. Just being on the boat was enough excitement for everyone, for an hour.

Now, from his position on the balcony, Copps recognized the lean figure and coppery head of the man he had just been talking to, Lenny Kollberg, the manager, walking back from the dock, then, after a look around, disappearing into a stand of young cedars that enclosed and shielded from view the camp generator and the log pile. Copps, on the balcony, could look over the cedars to where Deborah Wilkie, whom Copps had seen at breakfast with, presumably, her husband, waited. Kollberg appeared, she spoke, Kollberg spoke in turn, she nodded, they moved closer under the cedars, kissed, and he turned and disappeared into the lodge. As he left, Deborah Wilkie emerged from the trees and resumed her stroll towards the cabins.

"Well, well," Copps said, to himself. "Well, well, well. Like being on board a cruise ship. The purser gets his pick." There had already been some curiosity among the guests about Kollberg, and the absence of a wife, or apparent girlfriend. "That answers that," Copps said, to himself. He found Deborah striking: ordinary brown, frizzy hair (already mixed with grey) and a nice tan, but with blue eyes that lit up her face and demanded comment.

The departure of all the children made the world a different and quieter place. The camp workers not needed on the picnic had been given a day off, and they packed into the cars that a few of them owned and drove to the town for a little shopping and to eat some Asian food, curry or Chinese, something the cook never provided at the lodge. In ten minutes the boats were out of sight and the lodge had gone quiet and only Brendan Copps was waiting for Bert Tyrell to appear and guide him.

The wet nose of a dog pressed itself against Copps' ankle, and from the beach Bert Tyrell waved that he was ready, that it was his dog sent to bring him.

Copps followed the dog down to the beach to meet his guide. That was what the manager had told him to do. "Bert's a bit of a character," Kollberg had said, "but he knows the country. He's our oldest inhabitant."

"How old is he?"

"God, who knows? More than eighty, that's for sure. Maybe closer to ninety. I'm not kidding."

"Does he have to work?"

"He's got a daughter in the city who wants him to come live with her. But he says here is where he lives. I'm glad to have him."

"Why? Local colour?"

"That, too, but mainly because he can fix anything mechanical. You know those people—well, you hear of them— who look after wounded animals? They live surrounded by three-legged dogs and ducks with broken wings, nature's handicapped? Bert is like that with machines. Anything mechanical breaks, he'll figure out how to fix it. Without him we'd have to be bringing in a mechanic from the city whenever something goes wrong. Last summer he even fixed an electrical game machine, one of those video games, the kind I don't understand enough even to play. The man is a genius. A natural. I thought you'd enjoy him."

Now Copps caught it, under the American tones, a hint of another accent. Scandinavian?

He said, "Kollberg? Swedish?"

"German. I was born near Sioux Falls, South Dakota, in a very small enclosed community of Mennonites, so perhaps you still hear that in my voice." He nodded and walked off.

The honeymooners paddled their way with rough rhythm into the middle of the quiet lake. The girl rested her paddle across the canoe. Over her shoulder, she said, "This day needs superlatives…"

"Not yet. Not for me." The boy continued paddling firmly.

"It will. Don't worry, Simon. It will, it will, it will. But not if you worry. It was in a movie I saw about treating polio. Thinking doesn't help. In fact, it gets in the way."

After some time, he said, "Don't think I'm worried. Concerned, yes. But patient. Maybe even 'Concerned Patient'."

Another long pause before she said, "I must admit, I never expected anything like this, though my grandmother…"

"What else is like this?"

An even longer pause. "You're being aggressive. Don't be." She started paddling again. "Do you think being the son of a minister is the reason?"

"You asked that already. If that were the case there'd be a name for it. 'Vicar's Droop'. Something like that. It isn't my narrow Puritan upbringing, I can tell you. Both my parents were keen to keep me free of the tensions of each stage of growing up as it arrived. Father explained to me about masturbation long before I needed to know; then he explained all the other pitfalls, roadblocks and general hazards as he believed I was coming up to them. My mother helped. No one was better prepared to move smoothly into adulthood than I. If they had been classically repressive, then I might have been the equally classical vicar's son—you know, the vicarage letch, tupping all the farm girls in the parish—but maybe the same psychology worked in reverse. Understanding all, I decided to dedicate myself to the woman I would marry. She turned out to be you. I didn't expect what happened next. It was the one thing Father didn't warn me about."

She said, "I thought it might be me. You know." She trailed her hand in the water, feeling the top few inches already warm, and underneath, the coolness the summer had not yet penetrated. She slipped off her shirt to reveal her bikini.

"Look," he said.

They were approaching a small headland and a bird he didn't know flapped its way across the lake and into the sky.

She said, "That looks like a stork. That's a good sign. And that's the place I was looking for. Go into that little creek. We'll be the first today. It'll be our creek."

He stabbed the water harder, reaching down deep to get quickly to the mouth of the inlet. Inside there was no breeze, and no sound; the creek was reed-filled, the water glassy-smooth. The surface of the river seemed to be newly calmed, dusted with pollen, waiting for them.

She said, "O, Brave New World."

He said, "Some figures of speech are so old you don't realize that's what they are."

"Like 'O Brave New World'? That's what Miranda says when she sees Ferdinand. See, I feel like Miranda…"

"I know, I know. I KNOW. No, sorry, no, look, see, 'They cut through the water'. That's what I meant. That's what we're doing. 'Cutting through the water'. Am I being banal?"

"Probably." She pointed to the other shore. "Over there. That little beach."

He put his paddle across his knees, and trailed his hand in the water as she took over managing the canoe. "Should we swim?" he asked. "We'll have to wait until tomorrow morning to experience the water like this again."

"No."

"But isn't it too early for lunch?"

"For lunch, yes, it is. So keep paddling. When we reach that little beach I'll get into the water and pull us up."

As the canoe touched the sand she stepped carefully over the side, found her footing, pleased that the rubber shoes she was wearing worked as well in water as on land. Then she hauled the canoe up the beach. He started to hand her the ice-box, but she ignored it. "Just the blanket," she said.

"Ah, yes. Something to sit on." He tucked the blanket under his arm and they walked up the beach to the beginning of a path through the young cedars. She led the way knowingly for about a hundred metres uphill to an escarpment overlooking another, smaller lake.

"Here," she said. "This must be the place. It'll do, anyway. Put the blanket down."

He cleared away a few small rocks and secured the corners of the blanket with four flat stones. When he turned back to her she was undressed and lowering herself on to the blanket.

He hesitated, then kicked off his shoes and his jeans and shorts. As he began to wrestle with his T-shirt she pulled him down and kept him still while she stroked his back under his T-shirt. Slowly, knowingly himself now, he began to move. Innocence had kept them apart; now tenderness contrived with desire to bring them together.

Afterwards, she said, "Joe Littledeer told me about this place when I arranged the canoe. He said nobody will be picnicking here at ten in the morning except us."

"Did Joe Littledeer know what you had in mind?"

"Oh, I think so. But he didn't wink or anything. Thank the Ojibwa in him."

After the wedding, a civil ceremony conducted by a very nice woman and attended by two friends, they had eaten a wedding breakfast of pancakes and maple syrup at the Lakeshore Inn, said goodbye to their friends, walked about the town, eaten another meal at the same inn and finally stayed the night in a "Bed and Breakfast" house. The next morning they drove to the lodge where they had now been for three days. He knew himself to be totally and profoundly in love but they had continued to experience only frustration, until now.

Now, in their creek, they swam, made love again, then took the canoe to explore the rest of their backwater, seeing no one, hearing nothing except a loon calling, coming back to make an early lunch and to fall asleep in the afternoon shade. She woke up to find him grazing on her face, detail by detail. She said, "Now, I suppose you'll be insatiable."

"It looks like it."

"Tell me, Simon, have you never, really... No, let's change the subject. Tell me about your work. When did you first realize that you wanted to be a philatelist?"

"Philologist, airhead. Nothing to do with stamps."

"Whatever. Tell me about it. Start from the beginning."

"One thing: what were you starting to say about your grandmother? Sounded as if she gave you some classic pre-nuptial advice, for those days. What was it: 'Close your eyes and think of England, or rather, Canada'?"

"You've become a lot more sophisticated in the last couple of hours, haven't you? No, she told me about a man she knew, one of her crowd at college when she was dating, who didn't—couldn't—make love for the first week of his honeymoon, but it turned out all right. I think she told me that so that if it happened to us I was not to worry. The man's still alive. I know him."

"Now you can go back and tell Granny that it only took me four days."

Lenny Kollberg, the manager, said to Deborah Wilkie, the wife of the local real estate agent, a guest at the lodge, "Stay in your cabin while the picnickers get away. I'll come to you there."

"You will not. Find somewhere else. Just in case."

"In case of what?"

"Let me think. Roger will get to town and try to buy something and find he doesn't have his credit cards so he will phone the lodge here and ask that someone go to his room and make sure his wallet is there and there we'll be. Something like that. Okay?"

"Cabin Eight, then. It's not booked today. I'll call you when the coast is clear."

"Why would you be going in to Cabin Eight? I mean, if someone sees you, won't they wonder? Especially if they compare notes with whoever saw me going to Cabin Eight earlier. Someone might have. No, here, make it here. That way I can call you on my mobile if something goes wrong."

Herbie Wengler, like Bert Tyrell, was one of the lodge's originals. He had been at the lodge as long as anyone could remember. Originally, in his late teens, he had been hired as a storekeeper, but he wasn't very bright and he was anally retentive about the stores—he spent his days counting to make sure he knew exactly what he was in charge of; in fact, every day for Herbie was stock-taking even if he didn't call it that. They tried to make a guide of him, but though he learned his way around the rivers and lakes until he knew them almost as well as the guides from the reserve, and though he had no problem finding his way in the bush when he joined one of the pulp-cutting crews in the winter, he seemed incapable of simple tasks, like organizing the shore lunch, at that time a crucial part of a guide's day. (Creating shore lunch had involved getting a fire going, boiling a pot of water to heat the canned vegetables the guides were provided with, heating a mix of bacon fat and butter to fry the pickerel fillets, then making coffee.) Herbie never got beyond the stage of making a fire, changing his mind endlessly about the perfect spot, disappearing into the bush for kindling for as much as fifteen or twenty minutes and returning with two or three twigs, the only suitable materials for lighting fires he could find in half an acre of untouched bush. A soft-hearted management tried him on a succession of jobs, always as someone's helper, until finally he had been found a role of his own, as a kind of janitor for the workers' quarters, keeping their sleeping quarters tidy and their washroom clean.

He had also taken on the responsibility of keeping the fish-hut clean. This hut was a plywood shed where the guides used to gut their catch as they came off the lake at the end of the day. The hut was fitted with a bench in which three holes had been cut; beneath each hole an industrial-sized bucket was placed to catch the heads and tails and guts of the fish as the guides scraped them in. The cleaned fish were then stored in the ice shed behind the lodge. At the end of their stay, the guests could take home their catch, packed in ice. Very few actually left with their own fish; but there were always plenty in storage to make up a suitable box.

In the days when fishing had been the lodge's purpose, sometimes three guides at a time would clean their fish, standing at the bench, while more waited their turn outside. And because carting away the buckets of fish scraps when they were full was nobody's job, they often overflowed, and the fish hut was permanently a stinking horror before Herbie was assigned to keep it clean. After he took over, it was still a place to be avoided, but the stench had been much lowered and it was possible to stay in it for the few minutes it took to clean the day's catch. Herbie got Bert Tyrell to put a pair of wheels on a garbage can so that he could empty the buckets into it and, last thing at night, when the guests were all inside, he hauled the garbage can around the shore to the old dock, emptying it into the lake where the gulls waited. The "trimmings," as Herbie called them, were always gone by the morning. Herbie had an obsession with tidiness and his obsession served the camp well.

When the camp started to have different needs, when, sometimes, only the centre bucket was necessary and even it was never more than a third full, of kitchen scraps mainly, Herbie took on other jobs, nearly all connected with the camp's sanitation and the disposal of waste—in fact he became the one essential element of the camp's waste disposal system. He had one flaw, and it never interfered with his work and was hardly noticeable. He liked to get drunk, ideally once a week in private and in his own way. He could ignore his need for weeks, but when the opportunity arose he savoured the indulgence.

On the day of the picnic he had learned that Cabin Eight had not been booked and was still empty. He had a bottle of something labelled "Canadian Port" in his locker and he looked forward to drinking it slowly all afternoon and sleeping it off enough to function by the time the picnickers returned, though the advantage of using Cabin Eight was that he wouldn't be disturbed even if they came back early.

He ate an early lunch of hot dogs in the staff dining room, and set off to collect his bottle and make himself comfortable in Cabin Eight. He took a groundsheet to cover the bedding:

his clothing was clean enough but he knew he smelled more or less permanently of fish.

Cabin Eight was a family cabin, and Herbie took the inner bedroom. He laid the groundsheet out on the bed, stretched out and took his first long, luxurious swallow. There was always that first few minutes, sometimes half an hour, while he waited for the kinks in his fidgety body to subside, but soon enough he woke from the first light doze, ready and able to settle into a real sleep. He took one more long swallow, and composed himself.

Picnics were not Roger Wilkie's bag, as he told anyone who asked. He would rather take the opportunity to look at the real estate possibilities in the town.

There were 'For Sale' notices representing seven or eight well-known real estate companies posted round the town, but Wilkie was the only agent who called himself a "local man." The other signs were all of larger companies, province-wide, or even national. Wilkie thus advertised himself as "The Man Next Door," the agent you can trust. This fooled very few townsfolk who wanted to sell their properties; stories about Wilkie's business methods were common gossip. If some of the deals he made were too well-known for him to be trusted by the town, in the near-boom of the last twenty years the buyers Wilkie had dealt with were almost all out-of-towners, city folk, and while his neighbours didn't trust Wilkie an inch, they were happy to have him find a buyer when they wanted to sell the family home. Wilkie was good at putting together city folk who wanted an affordable place where they could get away from it all with the local retiring couple who wanted to move to the city, to an apartment near their grandchildren, somewhere where they wouldn't have to shovel snow. Wilkie was happy to try to sell anything, from a five-room "cottage" with two docks and three boats, to an undeveloped plot on the bank of the river, ideal for the handyman who wanted to build his own place.

The last twenty years had been good to Wilkie. The real estate market in cottage country had prospered as it had in the city, and Wilkie had been quick to see how cheap some of the properties looked to city folk, even buying the occasional real bargain himself through a partner, and selling it for a hefty profit. His major coup had been the acquisition of a tract of lake front on which he had a contractor build four cottages of different styles which he sold even more easily than he had expected, and for more money than he had thought he would. As a result he was on the brink of his biggest deal so far, and he was nervous and excited by his situation; because Wilkie was no Duddy Kravitz but a small-town chancer who was smelling his first try at the big time.

And that morning he had discovered, or rather confirmed his suspicion, that he was a cuckold. Two things had come together to make this fairly clear; that morning he had overheard the assistant manager, Tommy Li, who he had observed was more or less in charge of the day-to-day running of the lodge, answer a question that Kollberg had asked, saying, "Cabin Eight isn't rented today, Mr. Kollberg."

This meant nothing to Wilkie until, on the way to the dock to meet his guide, he found the sun warm on his head and turned back to his cabin for a hat, and saw his wife, Deborah, slip into the trees that screened the lodge's generator and log pile from the rest of the buildings. And then coming back from the hut he saw Kollberg slip into the same clump of trees and knew immediately that he was seeing what he had long suspected, and he started to make a plan. He detoured into the lounge, found Tommy Li, the assistant manager, at his desk and mentioned, just in passing, that he might be away all day and if necessary he would stay in town overnight. Would the assistant manager let his wife know? She didn't seem to be around at the moment. Then, making it a bit clearer, please tell his wife he would certainly not be back before dinner. And maybe not until the next morning. Okay?

At Wilkie's request they went in the guide's boat rather than by road. Wilkie, dressed in a business suit and tie as if expecting to find a customer at the lodge, wanted to have a look at the rest of the scenery, he said. It was several miles across Fergus Lake, down part of the river and out on to Marion Lake. The town was on the other side of this lake.

Wilkie met his guide at the dock and was helped into the boat. Wilkie was in his fifties but he was fat and far from nimble and Henry had to be careful getting him in.

Deborah appeared at the dock to see him off. At dinner the night before, she had told the other people at her table that she was not going on the picnic; she was looking forward to a day on her own, reading.

Brendan Copps watched her wave and start back up the path to the lodge. She stopped to exchange a word with Lenny Kollberg, who was standing outside the lodge, waiting to give the pontoon a final wave, and attend to any last minute problems. Deborah and the manager were too far away for Copps to hear what she was saying, probably the usual joke about the possibility of the boat sinking. Someone at breakfast had reminded everyone of Leacock's story of the Mariposa Belle. Now one of the guests on the boat called out, "All aboard for the Mariposa," getting a laugh.

A golf cart appeared, driven by a camp worker who was doing the rounds of the outdoor waste bins. Behind him, a camp worker with a spike on a pole scavenged for scraps of paper.

On board the pontoon, Winnie had got away from the old lady in the blue pantsuit and found herself a seat with her back to the wheelhouse so she could read or look at the lake if she felt like it. She wedged herself into a right angle made by the wheelhouse and the rail, making it difficult for anyone to sit next to her. Her most urgent need now was to avoid being trapped by Cassie Hepburn, whose bright grey curls she had seen and whose voice she had heard in the line behind her as they boarded. But she wasn't adroit enough. The voice said, "I saw you sitting alone and I thought you might be glad of some company now that you've managed to dodge that rude swine at dinner yesterday. I always bring a book, too, but I hardly ever get a chance to read it. Your husband not coming to the picnic?"

"He's not my husband and no, he's not coming to the picnic. He's going out on his own."

It was a mistake, trying not to be rude, thus adding the few words that might be taken as a conversation starter, some kind of invitation.

Mrs. Hepburn said, "I saw him on the dock. Is fishing included?"

Winnie looked at her now for the first time. "Included?"

"Is it an extra?"

"Brendan was going out with a guide, but I don't think he was going fishing. I assume he was paying for the guide and boat, though."

"And leaving you all alone."

Winnie looked around at the crowded deck. "Plenty of company here," she said.

"Mrs. Wilkie stayed behind, too, I noticed. Her husband was going to town, she told me," adding, rapidly, "By the way I don't think we were ever properly introduced. My full name is Cassandra but I shortened it in junior high."

Winnie adopted a smile that would let the other's chatter bounce off her. Eventually, after enough of her questions went unanswered, Mrs. Hepburn stood up and said, "You want to be left alone, I can tell. Probably had a fight with your policeman about this fishing thing. I'll be back." She made her way across the deck to a group leaning on the rail on the other side, camp workers who stood ready to dock the boat at the picnic site.

You're a rude bitch, Winnie said to herself. So she's a motor-mouth. As the bird-watching man said at dinner, that's not her fault. She's all alone and she's afraid if she stops talking she'll disappear.

She resolved to be politer the next time Mrs. Hepburn came around, for ten or fifteen minutes, anyway.

For, like Brendan Copps, she wanted to use the time and the opportunity of a week at the lodge to decide whether to marry. So far, and for several years, her life had been happily anchored by Brendan, but she was still not sure that she wanted to be absorbed completely into his life if there were too many unknown areas there. But as forty approached, so, too, did the need to anticipate the next stage of her life, say the next ten years. And the more she tried to anticipate the coming decade, the more it seemed to her that it was time to be married, or, at least, to be sharing her life with someone to the exclusion of everyone else. After that she expected the decisions would make themselves. In her experience, unions that survived into the partners' fifties tended to last.

She included in her future the possibility of a baby. She did not ache with longing, as at least one of her friends did, but one by one the disadvantages of being a mother—the shortage of money, the loss of personal freedom, the many possible disappointments, all of which she had witnessed among her friends—had all been anticipated, and been eventually outweighed by the sheer interestingness of the idea of bearing and raising a child so that now, at thirty-nine, late, but not uncommonly so these days, she felt herself open to the change.

The workers started to bustle as the island grew close. A large floating dock was permanently chained to trees on the shore, a dock big enough for the pontoon to tie up to, with a gangplank which everyone began to troop down.

Tommy Li, the assistant manager, went first, to help anyone who needed it onto the dock. Franny Taylor, the social director and Li's girlfriend, followed to corral the children who were now competing to be first off the boat and onto the beach. It was the job of these two to keep everyone happy until three o'clock. Packing up, a last game of horse-shoes, then marshalling the children into the bushes for a final pee would fill the time until the boat returned to take them home.

"You need any help?" Tommy asked Franny. The adults had found places to put their tote bags, sun hats, and cushions. One man was already in the water; two women walked off to explore what they could of the rest of the island. Soon Tommy would encourage the men to start kicking a ball about.

"I don't think so," Franny said. "I think I've got a professional babysitter helping out." She pointed to where Mrs. Hepburn was ordering the children to choose a piece of paper from those in her hand, all with numbers from 1 to 5. "Look at it, but DON'T TELL ANYONE YOUR NUMBER! Then form a circle, a ring, and close your eyes!"

"See?" Franny said. "I'm in luck. Here, today, anyway."

"How long you bin workin' at the lodge, Joe?" The outboard motor was noisy enough so that Wilkie had to shout.

Henry looked up from watching a loon guide her family away from the approaching boat. "Huh?" he asked.

Wilkie repeated the question.

"My name's not Joe. You got me mixed up." He stretched his leg to kick the gas tank out of the way.

"You got a family name, or does your tribe all have the same name?"

"It's a band. Not a tribe. And we have lots of different names. Like white guys."

"That right? What's yours?"

"Henry."

"No, I mean your other name. Your tribe name."

"Hyacinth."

"Hyacinth? Hyacinth? Like the flower? Hyacinth's a funny name for a guy, even an Indian."

"My granddad said the nuns gave it to us, so it's not my real name. Anyway, Hyacinth don't sound funny to me. I'm used to it. Wilkie sounds funny to me."

He concentrated now on taking them through a patch of roughish water as two currents came together. Emerging into the next lake he swung the boat in a violent arc, then back again. Wilkie grabbed both sides of the boat and hung on.

"Watch out," Henry said, and did it again. "The water's low," he said. "Lotsa rocks."

Wilkie spoke again. "So, what's it like, Henry? Up here. At the lodge. They treat you good? Henry? You hear what I'm saying?"

"Sure I can hear you. Whaja mean, 'You hear what I'm saying'? I'm not deaf, for fuck's sake. What are you saying?"

"I mean, how do you like your job? Working for the lodge, taking guys like me fishing."

"I don't work for the lodge. This is my own boat."

"How's this Kollberg guy to work for?"

"I don't work for Lenny Kollberg. I told you, I own this boat. You got a lot of questions, mister. What else you want to know? What time you want to be picked up?"

There was a silence for several seconds. Then Wilkie said, "And fuck you, too, Hiawatha, or whatever your fucking name is. I'll find my own way back. So what do I owe you?"

"You pay at the lodge. And the name's Hyacinth, Henry HyaCINTH. Nobody here called HiaWATHA. Where'd you get that name?"

David, Henry's brother, paddled his guests slowly through the narrows that connected the main channel with another smaller channel that flowed parallel. He had shut down the motor and was using a paddle in order to keep the world quiet as his guests searched the scene for the birds they had come to see. David normally only used his paddle when they were fishing for bass, or when his engine broke down, which never happened. But the fourteen-foot aluminum boat wasn't designed for paddling and it was hard work. His guests today regularly asked to be allowed to do a turn at the paddle, but David said no. They would stop for lunch soon and after they had eaten would be the time to maybe let the man have a little turn. Maybe, too, the wife would get sleepy or worried about sunburn and they would call it quits. Bird watchers made a nice change from fishermen and so far these people had been easy to work for and they looked good for a decent tip, but David would be perfectly happy if they wanted to quit early, as long as he got his day's pay.

"God Almighty," Donner said. "Look at that."

High on the other bank a wall of rock loomed up, to a city person, about four storeys high. Three storeys up, a ledge ran around the cliff, and on top of the ledge a moose was scrambling to find a path down the rock face. Now it was trying to turn around on a ledge the size of a windowsill. The objective of the moose was to get to another ledge twenty feet below where its calf was stuck on its own ledge; there was no obvious path connecting the two ledges.

"Can't we do something?" Mrs. Donner asked, leaning forward anxiously, the tips of her fingers in her mouth. "Can you get a bit closer?"

"We can stay out of the way while we tell the guys responsible, see how they figure it out," David said, a mobile phone in his hand. He dialed a number and started to talk to someone called Raymond, reporting the incident. When he snapped the phone shut, he said. "That moose weighs half a ton. More. You don't want it to fall on you. I called the department. They'll send a plane to take a look."

They left the moose behind and carried on through the narrows into the second stream, then, "Look," Donner said. "There! There!"

A large blue bird was standing still in the shallow water at the edge of the lake. As they watched, it dipped its head suddenly and came up with a fish that it manoeuvred in its beak until it could swallow it head first. Then, perhaps seeing them, it rose clumsily then gracefully into the sky and disappeared. "There it is, the great blue heron," Donner said, satisfied. "Are you getting pictures, Joanna? We've never seen one before."

David said, "There's plenty of them around. They're no good to eat."

Mrs. Donner was clicking rapidly, her camera up to her eye. "I think I got everything," she said.

"Then let's have lunch," Donner said. "I've had enough excitement for one morning. We've been lucky. Do you have to start that motor, David?"

"I could paddle across to that little beach over there," David said. "It'll do. The lunch is all packed. They even gave us hot coffee."

"Let's do that, then. We'd like to savour the moment but that motor of yours rather interferes."

The Donners were vegetarians, and the lodge had put together some egg sandwiches and added a banana and some oatmeal cookies. There was a ham sandwich for David.

Half an hour later, while they were resting after their lunch, a float plane passed overhead.

David said, "That's them. I wonder how they'll make out with the moose?"

Donner conferred quietly with his wife. To David, he said. "Do you know a long way round, to get home, I mean? We've had enough excitement for one day but it's still early."

"Sure. We'll be going with the current so it'll be easier. I'll paddle us back as far as that narrows, see how those moose made out."

Mrs. Donner said, "But…"

She need not have worried. When they reached the rock cliff there was no sign of the moose or her calf.

"They got down the rock somehow, and swam to somewhere safe," David said. "Or they didn't." He grinned.

"I hope they are all right. But it was nothing we did, was it?"

"Perhaps we'll hear about it from someone else," Donner said. "Home, David."

"But what will happen if those animals have fallen down the cliff and hurt themselves?" Mrs. Donner wanted to know.

"The band will pick them up and have a barbecue," David said. "Last year one of the band come across a deer that had been hit by something as it was crossing the road. Still alive but its legs was broke. Fed a lot of people, that deer did. And the guy who found the deer sold the head to a shop that stuffs them. He kept the skin for hisself."

Later, back in their cabin, Donner said to his wife, "You know that story David told us about how his band made a feast out of the deer they found. Do you think he made it up?"

"Made it up?"

"Yes. I've had the feeling with a few of David's anecdotes about the life here that he's telling us travellers' tales. You know, incidents he's polished up, he's told them so often."

"They are interesting, though, even if they aren't quite true."

"I think that's the point. Freud said the same thing about his theories."

Deborah Wilkie took what she hoped would look like a casual stroll around the lounge, then passed through the door marked 'PRIVATE' to the staff quarters. All of the managerial staff were out, busy with the picnic, except the manager himself. She checked the other three staff bedrooms anyway, knocking on the doors, ready with a made-up request for information. Finding no one home, she moved on to Lenny Kollberg's room. His door opened immediately and she slipped in and pulled it shut behind her, locking it. "I was right," she said.

"There's a couple of old guys in Cabin Twelve, playing cards. I saw them through the window."

"They see you?"

"What's to see? Just one of the guests walking by the window."

He kissed her on the cheek and crossed the room to close the curtain on the window that overlooked the back road. When he turned back she was under the duvet, shivering slightly. Kollberg piled his own clothes on the chair beside the bed and paused to lean over and kiss her properly, to stop her shivering. She reached out, her eyes closed, and pulled him onto her.

They were done in a few minutes. It was always that way the first time; it was the second time, fuelled by Kollberg's peculiar stamina, that she anticipated.

They talked, waiting, about the season the lodge was having, and about her life in the city, as her husband's unpaid housekeeper and bookkeeper.

After the second time, she said, "That felt like a good one. For you, I mean. Was it? You really brought it off, didn't you?"

He said, "With you there aren't any bad ones."

"Baby," she laughed and smacked his bottom lightly. "I bet you say that to all your women. When do you want to see me again?"

"What do you mean, 'baby'?"

"Listen, a line from a movie that was never made. 'With you there aren't any bad ones, Baby'. Sounds like Humphrey Bogart and Lauren Bacall. You know? Never mind. So, when do you want to see me again?"

"That's a funny way to put it. When I come into town, in about three weeks. I'll call you ahead."

"No, I'll call you in two weeks, see if you know the date. I never know when he's going to be home. And no emails, not even cute pretend-advertising ones."

"I thought my last email was ingenious."

"If he finds out, he'll get ugly, and I'm not ready for that yet."

"So, I'll ask you again. When will you be ready?"

"You really mean that, don't you. It's not just this." She patted the bed beside her. "But I don't have any money. Not pocket money—he gives me that; I mean running-away-with-my-lover money. I'm too old to live in a garret."

"I wish it didn't matter, but the alimony takes most of mine."

"So. Me and Madame Bovary. You know that story?"

"No. Will you ever be? Ready to take off?"

She turned and looked at him without speaking for a few seconds. She sat up and arranged a pillow behind her. "Lenny," she said, "I told you, I'm trying to get some advice. Women, even farm wives, I hear, have more rights to a share of the property than they used to. I've contacted a lawyer in Winnipeg, and I'm going to see him next week. The thing is, I don't have particular complaints. Roger's not abusing me: a quick pop-in about once a month, and I hardly know he's been home. He doesn't actually hit me—he wouldn't dare. I look after his office and do all the typing, and I keep the house clean. And I don't even have to cook since he bought the O'Kum Inn; we eat there all the time. But my name isn't on any of the ownership papers. We need to be clear, Lenny, love. I don't want to feel guilty about misleading you—well, us misleading each other, I guess. Do you have any money I don't know about? No? That's what I assumed. That's what was clear the last time we let our hair down and I had to help you out with the hotel room. Therefore, Lenny, old boy, what we are doing has no future for me, even as a kept woman. And I'm concerned about the future, my future."

"Does it matter that much? We could just take off. Maybe we could start a bed-and-breakfast in Kenora. Someplace like that. Listen, Debbie, now's the time to say it, I've never been so sure of myself with a woman as I am with you. That a funny way to put it? I mean it."

"Let me talk to this lawyer first, find out all my options. Living with Roger Wilkie has been bad enough and it is getting worse, but I want to be leaving him for something else. At my age it's too late to do it for love. Why couldn't we have met twenty years ago?"

This was putting it more clearly than she had ever done before: Kollberg had no future to offer her and she could not commit herself to a man like that. Kollberg's contract at Dempsey's was for eight months, a longer term than any of his staff but still not quite a year's work. For the remaining four months he was dependent on his brother in Florida who managed a large motel in Captiva, and who regularly found a spot for Kollberg in the winter as assistant night manager. But there was nothing permanent about this job, either.

"Not much room for romance, is there?" Kollberg said, trying for lightness.

"We've been round that one, too, Lenny. This is not about romance, me and you, or not just about romance. It's about being lonely, or, rather, about not being lonely when I'm with you. It's about being wanted. It's about enjoying being in bed with you. Now that we're talking, let's be honest. I can't risk screwing up with Wilkie yet, until I know what I've got. I think I've been unlucky, winding up with him, but here I am. Being married to Wilkie is the only security I've got. If I stick with him a little longer, I might be all right in my old age. I wish I liked him more, but there it is. If you had any prospects it might be different, but any new owner could have you out of here in a month. We're having a good affair, both of us. And I don't feel lonely when I'm here. I'm trying to be hard-headed."

Her eyes were wet. This was as close as she could get to the truth. She did not want to hurt him, but when she contemplated the unlikely possibility that they would be free one day to—what?—to live together? The prospect was—well—worrying. But she was very tired of feeling uncertain about the future.

"It's about other things, too, I hope," Kollberg said. "I mean, for you as well as me."

"I said that, didn't I? Yes, that, too, for me, for sure, sometimes. I think about you a lot, Lenny, and when I catch sight of you by accident in the distance it makes me feel good."

"I'd still like to see a lot more of you."

"Well, you can't. So, do you want to quit?"

"No!"

"Nor do I, but I also don't want any more suggestions from you about taking chances." She sat up and wiped her eyes. "He's my support system. I'd have trouble making ends meet without him."

"You could always call me."

Now she laughed. "Lenny, my sweet, you have to save up to afford us a hotel room once a month."

"Okay, okay. Did you ever feel different about anyone?"

"Once, yes."

"What happened?"

"He died."

"From what?"

"Didn't I tell you? You want it all? I often think about him, too. Well, then, he committed suicide. Over me. After I told him I wouldn't be seeing him anymore."

"Why was that? Why didn't you want to see him?"

"Oh, I did, but I was trying to be practical, then, just as I am trying to be now. He wanted us to run away. I wanted to, too, but common sense prevailed and I didn't. I loved him, see, but I couldn't take him seriously."

"He must have been a bit unbalanced, to commit suicide."

"Of course he was. I unbalanced him."

"Are you still mourning him?"

"He comes up in my thoughts from time to time, yes. Mainly in the morning before I'm really awake."

"But you've had other relationships?"

"Oh, sure. I was only eighteen then."

"But nothing like that boy. The others, I mean."

"No." She stood up, sniffed, wiped her nose, turned towards the door. "And I've been unlucky every time. Okay, here's the condensed version:

"I grew up in Oshawa, a place where they make cars and trucks. My dad worked in an automobile plant. I never knew him; he died in some kind of accident away from the plant, an accident that he brought on himself so there was no compensation. And no money for me to go to university, my mother being a homebody and needing support herself. So I had no training, no trade, no profession. So I did a lot of things, starting as a waitress, hostess-y things. The farthest I got was to be offered a job in Winnipeg, as hostess of a fraternal club, you know, like the Elks. But it wasn't the Elks and they didn't really have the money for a hostess, and I was still supporting Ma. Then the job disappeared, but one of the members offered me a job in town here, looking after the front desk of a motel. The Pines. Remember that?"

"It went bankrupt, didn't it?"

"That's right. I told you I was unlucky. Fast forward now for about ten years, more, and I'm managing the dining room of Gilbert's Hotel, just outside town. Which is where Roger found me and offered to take me away from all this. My hair was falling out and Roger sounded like security at last so I said yes, we got married and Roger got the unpaid secretary/housekeeper he was looking for, and I got what I deserved. Okay? Now, how shall I get out of here? Through the lounge?"

"Go out the back door. If you bump into any of the staff, ask them if there is a post-box. Otherwise go for a little walk and come back into the dining room from the outside. Any of the staff you meet there, ask them for a cup of tea."

"This all necessary? It's like a bloody play."

"It's for your benefit. And mine, I guess."

"Right, yeah. Here goes, then. Exit left."

Roger Wilkie went into the O'Kum Inn on Main Street and ordered coffee. He took a sip and found his way to the washroom where he unscrewed one of the several miniature bottles of vodka he was carrying, and swallowed the contents, a decent slug, and dropped the bottle back into his pocket until he could find a waste bin. From another pocket he took out a packet of mints and crammed three or four into his mouth, crunching them quickly into a paste before swallowing them.

Back in the restaurant, he sluiced some coffee around his mouth, and then finished the cup. The day's work could now begin.

"I'm looking for a lawyer," he told the waitress. "Davis and Lewicki, the company's called. Know where their office is?"

"They have their office in the Municipal Building, Mr. Wilkie," she said, recognizing him and the importance of being careful around him. "You gettin' a divorce?"

"No."

"Sorry. Just joking. Only Bill Davis handles just about all the divorces around here. He did mine. That's about all he does. You can see his office from that window. More coffee, Mr. Wilkie?"

"I've got an appointment with a man named Radford," he said.

"I heard they had a new partner. Must be doing well. The new guy mostly handles real estate, don't he?"

"Probably. How much do I owe you?"

"Dollar-fifty. On your tab?"

He was the owner but his bills and Deborah's went on a tab, most of which got charged to the expenses of running a real estate business.

He nodded and put down a quarter for a tip.

"Thanks. They're in the next block, on the left. When you finish, we have a special on meatloaf for lunch. Eight ninety-nine, includes veggies and potatoes. Oh, I guess you don't care."

"Where is this lawyer?"

"In the next block." She pointed the direction. "On the second floor."

In the lawyers' office, Radford, who was handling the sale, seated them around a small conference table and introduced

Wilkie to another lawyer, Jason Murray. In front of each of them Radford's secretary placed a copy of the contract. There was a pause, and Radford said, "I think we are here to sign what we've agreed, gentlemen, unless anyone has thought of something that we missed last time." He looked at the other two. "No? Then let's do it."

They all signed the four copies in front of them and passed them on. Jason Murray picked up his copies and left.

"Possession?" Wilkie asked, looking through the document.

"As of the thirty-first of the month. Virtually immediately. Friday."

"How do they hear it?"

"From me, I think. I'll come in Friday morning with the notice. I'll bring someone to escort Kollberg off the premises. You say you have someone who could take over?"

"I thought of doing it myself."

Radford leaned back. "Yourself? It's pretty—er—specialized work."

"Like yours, eh? If I fuck up, then I'll get some help."

"I see. Then you just call together the staff of the lodge and take it from there. It's the way it's done these days."

"I may run into Kollberg this afternoon."

"Stay away."

"I can't do that. I won't say a word—about this."

"It would be better if you didn't go back this afternoon, that's my advice, but if you have to, you have to." The lawyer turned back to his desk, to another file.

"I have to. But I'll save my piece until Friday. You know where I can rent a car in this place?" He knew the answer; it was a small town and he knew just about everything of its business that mattered. But he was playing a role now. The big man in town. Mr. Wilkie.

Radford said, "I think they keep a car for rent at the service station in the next block."

"See you on Friday, then. Looking forward to it."

Radford shook his hand without looking up.

When he was gone, Susan, Radford's secretary said, "What a turd! Why do you take him on?"

"Like Fagin said, or thereabouts, 'It is my living'."

Wilkie drove along the road around the bay, nearly seventy kilometres. It was almost two o'clock as he approached the outbuildings. He parked behind the fuel storage shed and walked in from there, wondering how to play it. It might be sensible, he thought, to do what Radford had said, stay away. In a couple of days the bastard will be gone. But Wilkie wanted to catch them, bare-assed, not go through endless accusations and denials.

The hell with it, he thought. The effect would be the same, just that the camp workers would see a very simple story and never believe any other. For them Kollberg would have been fired because he was caught humping the new owner's wife. So be it. There was more satisfaction this way than there would be if he had to wait until Friday.

Cabin Eight was not yet made up. The new guests would not be arriving until late afternoon and the girls had left the cleaning of it until last. The door was open and Wilkie let himself in and locked it behind him. Hearing them fumble with the lock would give him time to prepare his face. He arranged a chair with his back to the door so they would seem to surprise him when they came in. Before he sat down he moved the fire screen aside and poked the pile of ash in the fireplace to uncover some still red embers that glowed as the air reached them. He laid a few sticks of kindling across the coals, added a couple of logs and lowered himself into the chair. He took out a miniature of vodka, disposed of it in two swallows, put the empty bottle into his pocket and lit a cigarette, ignoring the sign that told him he should not smoke. He was enjoying himself now. He felt a little dozy, but the rattle of the doorknob would wake him up; he was sure of that. Besides, it wouldn't be bad to look as if he'd been sleeping, would it? This was like writing a scene in a movie. He felt the discomfort of something like indigestion begin under his ribs, although he had been too excited all day to eat, even after he left the lawyer's office, which seemed now to be a mistake. The discomfort turned into pain and filled his chest and wiped out all other sensations before it disappeared.

"They've quit," Brendan Copps said. He reeled in his line.

"Wanna go for a ride? Look around the neighbourhood?"

"Not much. It's peaceful without that motor. I was only fishing for fun, anyway. What the hell does that sign mean?"

"'Fish for fun?'"

"Yeah. I've seen it in a couple of places."

"It dates from a time when we was all scared of eating the fish around here because of mercury poisoning. I still am. I'll paddle us a-ways, now. I'm all rested up."

"Hold on. You mean this lake's poisoned?"

"I mean people said the river system was once. I don't know if it still is or if they still say it. I don't take any chances. I don't like eating fish, anyway, never did. I don't like catching them, killing them, or eating them. Now, back to work. I have to earn my pay, not like you lot, retired at forty-five, is it? Like the army?"

"Want me to do some paddling?"

"Not necessary. You're paying, remember? Tell you what, you entertain me with tales of your experiences in the gallant Mounties."

"I'm in the O.P.P."

"Right. Sorry. The brave-hearted Ontario Provincial Police, then. They'll do. Tell me about the time you faced down three killers and all you had was a Swiss Army knife and a walking stick."

"I'll tell you about the afternoon I found myself alone in a boat with a mad old coot and I'd left my gun at home so I had to keep him off with a fishing rod."

"That'll do, too." Tyrell said, nodding. When no more response was forthcoming, he said, "You like being a copper?"

This wasn't a casual query, to be answered without thought. They were alone. The afternoon, the boat, the absence of company, had all created the conditions for daydreaming, and for asking questions and giving answers with no one to overhear, a place where the truth might be told.

"I did like it."

"What does that mean?"

"It means I'm thinking about your question."

"Did you dream about yourself being a copper when you were a little kid?"

"I don't remember that far back. When I was a big kid I dreamed about being a robber, not a cop."

"You serious? One of the mob, you mean?"

Copps gave himself plenty of time before deciding to reply. "There were four of us in the gang. In Grade Eleven. We started out stealing from supermarkets. We nearly got caught, so after that the store managers knew us. Then we concentrated on cars. You'd be amazed how many women leave purses in unlocked cars. We took anything they left behind."

"You okay telling me stuff like this?"

"You might ruin my reputation, you mean? You tell anybody, I'll just say I was bullshitting you."

"Right. And so you might be. What did you do with the stuff you stole?"

"Sold it. To a guy in Crampton, who we think unloaded it in Winnipeg."

"What happened? Why did you stop?"

"I grew up, I guess. Realized I had too much to lose. One of the gang, Smokey Stover, got caught, and the rest of us quit."

"What's happened to the rest of the gang?"

"One of them is a lawyer; another one is a bush pilot. And then there's me."

"Which one is Smokey Stover? That name takes me back."

"None of those. Smokey is currently serving seven years for armed robbery. Could have happened to any of us."

"Bloody hell. So what's the next step for you? Promotion to inspector?"

Brendan took his time, about to voice something that had been unspoken until now. "I'm thinking of quitting the force. Don't tell the world."

"To do what?"

Brendan lay back against the gunwale. "All right, I'll tell you. I started life on a quarter section of land my dad had inherited from his dad. I grew up planning my escape— anything but farming, I thought. I got as far as enrolling in engineering at the university, the usual way out then for a Saskatchewan farm boy if he completed Grade Thirteen, but I never graduated. In those days, ambitious boys wanting to avoid the farm they were from usually went into engineering. Sometimes, if the family had two good crop years in a row, then the boys might look to study agriculture to see if they could make the current prosperity permanent. Not me, though, not then. I was the kind of farm boy who grew up dreaming about the city. But engineering wasn't right for me, either—I had to get special help to pass first year math. So I found myself in the O.P.P. And very happy, I might say. Until now."

"Until now. So what's next?"

"You know the old saying, 'You can take the boy from the farm, but you can't take the farm from the boy'?"

"We didn't have sayings like that in Tooting Broadway. Go on."

"It means that if you grow up on a farm you'll always have straw in your hair. And cow-shit on your boots. Metaphorically, that is."

"And what does that mean?"

"It means it's true, but not in the way it's usually meant. For me, it means that I'm circling back, thinking maybe I really do belong on a farm, one of my own. A different kind of farm. A small one. A mixed farm, with maybe a stable of horses, and our own honey. You know?"

"No, I don't know. We kept some chickens in the back garden during the war but that was as close as I've ever got to a farm. I think you're daydreaming. You know anything about horses? More than me?"

"I'm comfortable around them."

"That's something, I suppose. I'm not. And bees?"

"Bees I'd have to find out about." Copps was tempted at this point to mention Winnie, who seemed to be there, in the pictures in his head, but he didn't want to say how much he had been thinking about all this.

Tyrell said, "You ain't married?"

"No." Once again, Copps stepped back from discussing this area of the future.

"You never been married?"

"No."

"That's not so unusual these days, is it? Lots of poontang round your way these days?"

Copps stared at him for a few moments, absorbing the quaintness of the term. Then he laughed. "I've just not met the one woman who is worth giving up the others for." He took a breath. "Until now, as a matter of fact. Until now. Now I'm forty, not so wide awake at night as I used to be, you know? And besides—and if you don't keep this to yourself I'll throw you in the lake, see if you can swim, even at your age—as I say, besides, I think I'm in love. For the first time in my life. I must have known fifty women—more—but I never said the magic words to any of them. I began to think I never would, and then I met this one."

"You love her?"

"That's what I'm saying. Yeah. I do. Yeah, I love her." It was a relief to be able to say it, even to an old man in a fishing boat on a river in Northern Ontario.

Tyrell turned his creased, whiskery old face on his passenger. "Coo, luvaduck. That's a confession, that is. Your secret's safe with me, mate. But wait a minute, you came up here by yourself, didn't you? To the lodge, I mean."

"I brought her with me."

Tyrell searched in his head for the faces of the current guests. "Winnie?" he said. "That the one?" Receiving a nod, he said, "Then you did well. She's a real lady."

"Too good for me?"

"As you tell it, yes. No cow-shit on her boots. But that's all right. You got lucky. She know?"

"I haven't told her."

"Yeah, but does she know?"

"I don't know."

"Tell her." Tyrell had now set aside all of his playful character, honouring the moment. "Good luck, mate. Being married was good to me. I wish you the same."

"Thanks. Any other advice?"

"Yeah. Don't fart in bed. So do me a favour?"

"What?"

"Let me know how it turns out. I mean, if she says yes or no."

"I'll put a notice on that board they use to list the day's messages. And what about you? What's an old man with a cockney accent doing out here?"

"Me? I left home to see the world. This was as far as I got."

"And you got a job as a guide. Here? With that accent?"

"All the guests were Americans, then. I sounded just right to someone from Nebraska. Local colour, I was."

"But now you don't like fishing. Did you ever?"

"I did at first. Then I didn't. It came to seem cru-ell to me." He pronounced the word comically, but only to emphasize the seriousness of it. "I listened to these blokes, day after day: 'I had a four-pounder on the line, put up a terrific fight before I lost him'. On a good day we would kill twenty fish and it was more fun if they struggled a lot before they died. I got tired of it."

"I was told that fish have very low pain centres."

"Who told you that? And how low do the pain centres have to be for the fish to object to being caught?"

"Did you talk like this to all the guests?"

"No, silly bugger, I became the camp handyman, which suited me better."

"Any of the other guides feel like you about it? How about the Indians?"

"Leave the Indians out of it. They fish to eat, not to have fun. Let me tell you a story. Once, in the early days, I got assigned to a party, a husband and wife, who had been given a change of guide because the Indian they started with had seemed cruel. The woman, a nice lady, told me that they couldn't stand the way the boy dealt with the fish they caught—he was very new to guidin'—we were short-handed and at a very busy time—and these two were pickerel fishing. They were having a good day—and early in the year that could mean a lot of pickerel. Well, the boy knew they didn't want to keep the fish, so as they caught one he netted it, lifted it into the boat, then stabbed it and threw it back. They were shocked. He was spoiling a nice day's fishing by murdering the fish. The thing was, he had no experience of fishing as a sport. For him, fish was a form of wildlife, there to be eaten. If you weren't hungry you didn't go fishing. If you throw back the dead ones they get to be gobbled up by some other creature. But to his guests he seemed a bit casual."

"So he was fired?"

"No. No, Jack gave him another party the next day, and told one of the rest of the fellas guidin' to have a quiet word with him. That's all it took. After that he unhooked the fish and put them back in the lake. Gently. Like the rest of us. It wasn't his way, but if that was what they wanted, all right."

"They lived to be caught again, then."

"They still died, but the guests couldn't see it happening. But, yes. Or every once in a while you'd catch a pickerel, but before you could get it in it would be grabbed by a big northern."

"And so you quit guiding?"

"I became the camp handyman. I like it here. I couldn't go back now. I grew up in a place called Tooting. I had one ambition then, to get out of Tooting. But I'd read about this bloke called Grey Owl, really an Englishman like me—you heard of him?—I didn't hear he was not an Indian until after I got here. So I came to Winnipeg and got a job in an office—I used to work as a clerk for the railway back home—and then, oh, well, I heard they wanted a storekeeper at this lodge, Dempsey's—so I took it. In the steps of Grey Owl, like. When I came up here, I got one of the university students who worked in the summers to show me a bit about guiding. It wasn't hard to fake after a couple of tries, and then came the day when they were very short-handed and I got to be a guide for a day, and then I switched over from storekeeping to guiding. I've told the story so often I'll leave the rest to your imagination. But soon I got to not like killing fish for fun, but by then I was very useful to them here as a handyman, which I should always have been, even in Tooting. I belong here now, as much as anywhere. My daughter lives in a place called Oakville, near Toronto, and she wants me to go there to live, but what would I do? Her husband's a doctor, nice bloke, but it's not for me. "

Later, Herbie thought he had not actually got back to sleep when the outer door of the cabin opened and someone came in to the main room, shutting the door behind them firmly, not slamming but with no attempt at stealth. The cleaning girls? No. Too heavy-footed. Probably the two old guys, Marcel Pascal and Ted Revell, but why?

For the first five minutes there were sounds of the intruder moving around, then the scrape of a chair, then silence.

He waited for half an hour, then eased open the door a crack and saw a man he knew named Wilkie slouched in an armchair, apparently asleep. His jacket was on the floor beside him. This was a man who frightened Herbie (Herbie was wary if not actually frightened of many people, around the camp and in the town). Now he watched this man for a few minutes, then silently collected together his groundsheet and bottle of port and crept towards the main door. He wanted nothing to do with this man; just that morning the man had shouted at him to go find Henry so he could begin his day, and cursed him again when he could not find the Indian. Henry had appeared in the middle of Wilkie's abuse, telling Wilkie that he had been waiting by the boat, down at the dock, causing Wilkie to shout at Herbie, "Down at the dock. Did you look there?"

As Herbie stepped around the sleeping man he saw—he could not help seeing—the man's wallet three-quarters out of the inner pocket of the coat. Herbie was not a natural thief; he was a totally trustworthy employee with a fierce loyalty to the camp that employed him, and to the people whom he had learned not to be wary of, but this was different. He didn't take the wallet for himself, but as a way of getting back at someone who had frightened him. Herbie took the wallet, and let himself out the door, making sure that no one saw him on his way to his room. He planned to put the wallet in the little space in his locker behind the drawer where he stored his socks, and get rid of it later, but almost immediately he remembered a famous incident, ten years before, when the then manager had ordered the bunkhouse searched to look for a valuable wristwatch one of the guests had lost. They found the watch, and that was the last of that guide after the manager of the time had given him what Bert Tyrell called a "bloody good hiding."

Herbie knew that he was not up to keeping the wallet, and he considered just throwing it away, but then he thought if someone found it and took it to the police they might test it for fingerprints, and then as he was passing the fish hut he saw the answer. He slipped inside the hut and dropped the wallet into the centre garbage can, now about a quarter full of "trimmings," mainly spaghetti from yesterday's dinner, and watched as it slid under the slimy surface. There was no chance that anyone would disturb it before he emptied the garbage can into the lake, early the next morning.

He walked quickly back to his room, grabbed his windbreaker and trotted down to the beach where he kept his own boat, an old wooden, twelve-foot boat with a 9.9 Johnson outboard motor that a previous camp manager had given him. Sometimes he took the boat out for a little ride on his day off, but his chief pleasure in owning the boat was in keeping it clean and dry with all the parts—ropes, safety kit, anchor, life jackets—neatly ready for anything that came along, and with a full tank of gas. Now he untied it, stepped in, and headed for the channel that would let him out into the lake on the other side of which lay the town. He had been frightened more or less from the time he had opened the door of his room and seen the sleeping man until now, in the middle of the lake, but now he looked around for any other boats and saw he was alone and he calmed down as he headed across the lake to the town dock.

Henry Hyacinth called over to Herbie as he walked through the door of the café. The woman behind the counter held up a bottle of beer and Herbie nodded, and she pressed off the cap and brought the beer to the table. There were only two other men in the pub, both from the reserve. It was a tiny café, owned and operated by Henry's daughter, and it was patronized mainly by members of the band in town for the day.

"Herbie. You look like you've got a hair up your ass. What's up?"

For a moment Herbie considered telling Henry what had happened to him in the last hour. Henry was a big guy with hair down to his shoulders and missing several front teeth, but he had never frightened Herbie, and at the moment Herbie just needed someone to sit with, not to share his experience with. If he talked too much right away he would lose control of it. He should keep his mouth shut, for a while, anyway.

"Just came over for a boat ride and a look round the town," Herbie said.

"Fuck-all around here you haven't seen before."

Henry had spent the day giving himself a day off, touching bases, mainly calling on his daughter who lived above the café with a man who owned and drove the town's only taxi. She fed Henry lunch when he came to town. She was always glad to see him.

When Herbie walked into the café, Henry saw in him the man he had been looking for all afternoon, now stopping by for a beer, probably, before he went back to the lodge. "Herbie," he said. "I got a problem."

"Yeah?" Herbie liked the sound of this. At least it might take his mind off his own problem, relieve him from thinking about what was happening at the lodge, about what Wilkie would say and do when he woke up and found his wallet missing and what he, Herbie, would say when he went back about where he had been, and what he had been doing. He would have to be careful because someone might have seen him. He didn't think so, but they might have. So he had to have a story that would allow him to be seen leaving the lodge area and crossing the lake.

Money. He would say he had forgotten his money and wanted to buy something he had seen in town. What? He looked himself over. The only thing he needed was gloves. That was it. A good pair of work gloves, the heavy kind made of yellow leather like Marcel had. He had always meant to get a pair like that; now he would.

"I need a hand," Henry was saying. "I got a new stove from the lumber yard up near St. Charles. It's been delivered to the store in Clactonville, about ten kilometres up the road. I've found a guy to lend me a pick-up, but see, I don't drive…"

"I do," Herbie said. "I can drive a pick-up. They made me get my licence so I could drive the heavy garbage over to the town dump. I've always kept up my licence. I can drive standard and automatic, both ways. Where's the pick-up?"

"McMurtry's yard. I'll show you. You all set?"

The relief was temporary but enormous. "Can I have another beer first?" Herbie asked. "Then I've got to get me a pair of gloves."

The beer drunk, they called in at the hardware store and Herbie paid twenty dollars for a pair of yellow leather gloves, which he put on. "Got to get them broke in," he said to Henry, holding them up, and working his fingers.

The two men walked down the street to McMurtry's lumber yard and found the pick-up truck parked inside the gate.

The new stiff gloves made the act of shifting gears feel unfamiliar, as if he was just learning to drive again, but as soon as he turned on to the road and shifted into top gear, he felt fine. He drove them over to the hardware store.

The stove came from Sweden. It was made of thick steel.

"Can you guys manage it? It's a real ball-breaker," the hardware store manager wondered, standing well back, not wanting much to share in the lifting.

Henry Hyacinth was savvy about bull work, which he did a lot of when he wasn't guiding. "You got a dolly?" he asked the foreman. "Something with wheels?" he said. "We'll roll it over to the pick-up, then you..." he nodded to the foreman, "...can help us lift it up. I heard one of you guys saying the other day that us Indians are too light in the ass for heavy lifting. Maybe he's right. I gotta be careful." There was no expression on his face as he spoke.

It turned out to be simpler than Herbie feared. All of them, including Henry, knew how to lift heavy weights off the floor. At a nod from Henry the three men straightened up slowly and slid the stove on to the back of the pick-up. The storekeeper dusted his hands, looking pleased. "You going to tie it down?" he asked.

"You think the wind might catch it?" Henry responded. "Let's go, Herbie." A drop of rain fell on his hand. He looked up at the sky. "Fuckin' rain." He waved his thanks to the foreman. "Buy you a beer next time I come to town," he said, and they drove away.

By the time they reached the town, the sky had become heavy with the approaching rain. At the dock two acquaintances of Henry volunteered to help them get the stove into Henry's boat. "I'll buy you a beer next time I'm in town," Henry promised them automatically.

One of the helpers said, "Now would be a good time. By the way, you got a fire over to the lodge."

"That right?" Henry stared across the lake where smoke was hanging above the lodge area. "I guess we missed that, eh, Herbie? Never mind. What do you say to us having another beer before we go? We earned it. Yeah, you guys come, too."

The two men jumped on the back of the pick-up, and Herbie took them all back to the café. There, the beer consumed, Henry took a twenty from his wallet. "I owe you, Herbie," he said. "Here."

"You don't owe me," Herbie said, pushing the money back. "Not a goddam thing. I like to help." He pointed out the window. "The rain's stopped; it was just a shower."

"Good. I have to take that stove up to my place," Henry said, glancing at the sky through the window.

"Okay. Let's go."

It took the two of them nearly half an hour to get to the reservation and Henry's house. The stove was so heavy that Herbie was afraid that the sharp edges on the steel feet might cut his new gloves, and then he thought they might cut through the fibreglass bottom of the boat, so they had to balance the stove on the centre seat of the boat and Herbie had to sit leaning forward, his hand on it, to make sure it didn't slip.

At the beach by the reservation there were no men around to help them, and there was no real dock. Henry jumped out of the boat and hauled it up the little beach. Herbie got into the water, too, and they pushed and lifted the stove, first onto the side of the boat, then over onto the bench seat. Small gusts of rain were promising to soak them, but Herbie didn't care.

Henry's dog showed its teeth at Herbie, but Henry sent it back with a word.

They could manage about six feet at a time. Henry wanted to wait until another man appeared, but Herbie insisted they give it a go. The longer they stayed away from the lodge, the less chance that he would be connected with whatever was happening.

Eventually Henry hit on the idea of sliding the stove onto a sheet of plywood and dragging it up to his shack. That worked, but it was hard, and when they got to Henry's door, Henry said, "That's it, Herbie. You may not be but I am fucked. Let's have a beer."

"We'll make your house muddy," Herbie said.

"Yeah, I'll bring the beer out. We can sit on the porch."

They drank two bottles of beer each, and Herbie began to feel he was getting his weekly buzz after all.

Henry said, "Did you see what was on fire? It wasn't big enough to be the lodge."

"No," Herbie said.

"I guess we should go help."

"Let's have another beer, then, give them time to clean up," Herbie said. "I left my boat at the town dock."

Henry said, "I'll take you over to the lodge in my boat. You could get a ride back in the morning, pick your boat up then."

Herbie said, "I'm not leaving my boat there all night."

"Okay, then. I owe you, anyway, pal. Let's go get your boat."

Together they crossed the lake back to the town. Herbie let Henry off at the main dock and then carried on to the old dock where he tied up the boat. He took his time about walking back to the scene of the fire.

"Written anything lately, Mel?" Wayne Lucas asked.

They had enjoyed a good morning touring the river system, remembering the good spots. Matthew, the guide, had brought a vacuum flask of coffee after they had eaten their packed lunch and now they were waiting for a signal from him that he was ready to begin the afternoon. It would be at least another half hour, though, for after tidying up the campsite the guide rolled up his jacket for a pillow, laid down in the shadow of the boat, belched lightly, and composed himself for sleep.

Part of their time together was always given over to conversation about their other, private, writing lives. Like many professors of English, they had drifted into teaching, hoping, expecting, that studying literature would help them in their yearning to turn their experiences into stories. As with most of their colleagues, that hadn't happened, but the yearning hadn't entirely drained into the sand of the classroom, and sometimes one of them managed to publish a poem or a short story in a college magazine or in a competition run by a local newspaper, but it was getting harder and harder. In the case of Lucas, the poet, his problem was that he simply could not respond to the kind of poetry he saw published. He had spent a lifetime crafting the intricacies of sonnets and ballads, but form no longer seemed to matter, at least the traditional forms. The problem for Gladstone was that all short stories these days seemed to be written by the young about themselves, and their world seemed inaccessible. But together, once a year, the two old men talked about what Gladstone called "our embers," often stirring enough of a flame to try, when they got back home, to give it another go.

Gladstone said, "I am working on something but I don't know what it is yet. Maybe just a chapter of my long-awaited memoir." He pronounced the words solemnly, comically, to take away any suggestion of pretentiousness. Then, "I brought it with me. Want to hear it?"

"How long is it?"

"Five pages."

"I can manage that. Go ahead."

Gladstone lifted up the rain jacket he had brought and lifted out a typescript from an inside pocket. "Ready?"

"Go ahead." Lucas adjusted his shoulders to fit a large boulder.

"I haven't quite finished the ending…"

"Don't dick around, Mel. Just read it."

"Right. My best podium voice, then. Remember, I haven't polished it…"

"Read it, Mel. Read it."

Gladstone grinned, settled the paper in his hand, and pronounced, "Narcolepsy."

"What?"

"That's the title. Narcolepsy. It means…"

"I know what 'narcolepsy' means."

"Right. Here goes then:

Afterwards he realized that he had begun to register her from the time she started to pick her way through the small crowd around the perfume counter (it was Christmas), and watched as she crossed the space between them to where he was standing, waiting for Eleanor, at the foot of the "UP" elevator.

The face came immediately, but the name waited. She kissed him, not in salutation, but firmly, signally, on the lips, a real smacker, then said "Hello" in that breathy, slightly trembling way he had never forgotten, before she turned and disappeared back into the crowd.

"Who was that?" Eleanor, appearing now by his side, wanted to know.

"I'm not sure," he said.

"Of course you are."

"Of her name, I mean. Give me a second."

He was telling the truth. Her name was coming into his head now, but until he tested it aloud he would not be certain of it. Names were being everywhere elusive. It would come eventually, of course, perhaps on the way home, or in bed tomorrow morning. It was no longer even worth pursuing a letter through the alphabet.

"Someone from the office?"

"Ten years ago? Fifty? A long time, anyway."

"I guessed that much. No one I knew." She scrunched up her face like a child mildly regretful at being denied a treat. "Now, I need about half an hour. Buy yourself a coffee. I'll look for you at Starbucks." She pointed through the door to the coffee shop across the mall.

As soon as Eleanor left, the woman reappeared, walking quickly; she claimed another kiss, then turned and disappeared, this time for good. Afterwards he knew she did not flee for fear of the return of Eleanor. The message she wanted to convey was all there in the second kiss.

Now the name was waiting for him when he returned to it— Lucy, Lucy Turgeon. Someone he had taken home from a dinner party where he had offended the hostess (he learned later) by yawning all through dinner and afterwards until Lucy managed the conversation so that she needed a ride home and he was the best one to offer it.

At her house, she suggested coffee, though he was now wide awake. His narcolepsy was a recurring condition, happening once at a meeting of the lunch club he belonged to. He had arrived yawning, dozed off standing up over a pre-lunch glass of wine, and gaped all though lunch, remembering afterwards the phrase "Is he all right?" coming through the fog more than once. He remembered nothing more except being driven home by Fred MacDougal. There had been other incidents, attacks, really, some only the overwhelming need to close his eyes for a few seconds, but he had always been able to fake a few moments of deep thought. The phase had passed; he moved from narcolepsy to insomnia until it, too, receded, blanketed at first by Temazepam then cured by a change of job.

She was a divorcee now, with two children, a classic marriage wrecker in form but not in practice. Afterwards she said, "If I hear through Susan"—their hostess that evening—"that you have breathed a word to your wife, I'll make your life a living hell."

He had often wondered how she would go about it.

The house he drove her to belonged to a friend of hers; she had borrowed it for a short visit. She guided him through parts of it, not upstairs, *but down to the basement, to the recreation room where they made love on the grey shag rug in front of the television.*

And that, for fifty years, was that.

It was his first venture into adultery, and he was not sure what was expected of him, except for her warning, but he thought it went well. He never saw her again. The next morning, by cleverly managing a telephone conversation with Susan when he called to apologize for his poor manners the night before, he allowed the conversation to drift into an account of how he revived well enough to be safe to drive Lucy (a cunning pause here: is that her name?) and himself home. Susan said that she had called Lucy already and learned that he had deposited her safely on her doorstep. From Susan he got the name of the people who owned the house where Lucy was staying, looked for and found their telephone number, but when he called, he got an answering machine. Later, Susan told him that Lucy had probably already gone back to Vancouver.

He thought about her constantly, for a week, then intermittently, then only occasionally over the years, but he was never able to resolve the doubt that he had failed in some way. Not in the obvious way—what began in awkwardness and diffidence had ended with brio; nevertheless, he never stopped wondering if he hadn't shown himself deficient, inexperienced, undeveloped, untutored, a dance partner who didn't know the steps of a rhumba.

Why had she not stopped now, here? Why hadn't she spoken? Because she saw Eleanor, guessed who she was, and knew, as women did, that Eleanor would see that she was no old colleague, or childhood friend? So she had returned, not to talk, but just with a second kiss, one that made sense of the first, a kiss that said, yes, I meant it. To be kissed twice within minutes by a woman like Lucy Turgeon—no, by Lucy herself—what did that mean?

He ordered another cup of coffee and put himself to the task of figuring it out. He got as far as knowing the obvious, that the second kiss meant something if only that it confirmed the first. The possible additional interpretations—regret, a promise (surely too late for that), confirmation that their encounter still endured—all that if not more, the whole episode fifty years ago confirmed by the first kiss, itself now reconfirmed by the second.

That would be that, of course. The second kiss illuminated the memory, and allowed him to make his peace with it. If he had had such confirmation fifty years ago, his life might have followed a different trajectory, but now finally something unresolved had been resolved, and he was content.

But what about her? Perhaps the message was about her; perhaps something in her had been resolved at the sight of him, standing by the "UP" elevator. Perhaps the first kiss was all about her; then she had to return to share the discovery with him.

Yes, that was it.

"That it?"

"Well, yes. Do you think it's incomplete?"

"Oh, it's complete enough, as a story." Lucas adjusted himself against the boulder. "I don't believe it, though."

"Don't believe it? But it really happened, just like that."

"Oh, Mel. It really happened. Just like that?" Lucas laughed. "The old chestnut. No, what I meant is that you made up a bit, in the middle, there. About rogering her on the carpet. That's the bit I don't believe. Take that out and you'll have a story. "

"What about the rest? The kisses."

"Oh, that works. Yes, that's good. But not the rogering on the grey shag rug."

"I should take it out, then, the—what do you call it—the rogering?"

"Think about it. What do those two kisses mean? Where was it, by the way? Outside Holt Renfrew down in the mall? I mean the kissing, not the rogering. That, you say, took place on the grey shag rug."

"So why, do you think? She must have remembered something."

"Or thought she did. Let it cook, Mel. It'll come to you, by and by. Take out that rogering, though."

"So what about you?" Sarah Slocombe made an obvious effort by squaring her body to face Winnie, to show herself a listener to someone else's troubles. She and her husband, George, had flown from England to meet her new son-in-law, who had turned out to be a disappointment, or, in George's terms, a "bit of a shit" who had made it clear that he had no interest in his wife's family and did not intend to put himself out to please them. He was a writer and he spent most of his time locked up in his office, complaining about interruptions. After a week of rudeness on his part, anger on George's, and misery on Sarah's, they had sought an alternative way to spend the remainder of their holiday, and someone had recommended Dempsey's.

An apology of some sort had seemed appropriate, and Winnie had duly said she was sorry that Sarah's new son-in-law had turned out to be a disappointment. "Not all Canadians are like that," she added, in automatic reflex.

"He's not a Canadian," Sarah said. "He's from Bath or Wells, somewhere down there. He's actually a librarian trying to be a writer. Something to do with books, anyway. Very, very snotty. So, let's talk about something more cheerful. Do you mind if we sit on the other side? I'm getting sunburned." She pulled on a thin grey sweater. "I brought this in case of getting chilled. Silly me, but it will work for sun, too. Now. You. A professional with your own business, hitched to a real salt-of-the-earth chap; sounds like the good life to me," she said. "If that sounds as if I envy you, well, today I do."

"Oh, I don't have any complaints."

"Except."

"What?"

"Except what?"

"Except what? What are you saying?"

"Whatever's making you thoughtful. Whenever I've peered through my own veil of tears I've noticed you, very abstracted. What are you brooding about?"

Winnie looked around. The two women had found a spot to spread a blanket, their backs against a rock wall, the noises of the volleyball game, and of the children, agreeably distanced. "Brendan, of course," she agreed.

"He being a worry?"

"Not a worry, no."

"Sounds as though Act One is over. I'm a regular member of the Longborough Little Theatre. I used to play your part, but now I'm mostly 'Best Friend', or 'Understanding Aunt'. I often have good lines, though. Try me."

"Act Two is nearly over, too, and there doesn't seem much plot."

"Let's bring the curtain down, then. What do you want to happen in Act Three? What's the usual kind of happy ending?"

"Wedding bells—in your play, that is."

"But he's not interested? Maybe Granny was right: you let him have his wicked way before the night and now he doesn't have to marry you."

Winnie laughed, recognizing that this was a slightly clever way for her new friend to find out her status. "I don't think that's the issue."

"What then? You've found out about his other woman?"

"He's told me about her, or rather, them."

Sarah raised her eyebrows in wonder and glee, her own problems now quite set aside. "Fill me in," she said. "I mostly get *my* information from the telly, always ten years behind what is happening this season. This is the real thing. This is life. In Canada, anyway. Not Chipping Campden."

And this is shipboard stuff, Winnie thought. I'll tell you because I'll never see you again. "Okay. When I met Brendan, a few years ago, he made it clear that I wasn't the only one in his life. One thing about him, he's honest. But there's been no other woman for more than a year now, maybe a couple of years, and the implications of that are that I'm all he needs, and I've known for some time that he's all I want. How's that for a line for your next production? So where do we go from here? What am I to expect?"

"A handful of rice, surely, or the common-law equivalent. What about children?"

"I never even thought about them, and then I did. I've found in the last year that I would like one or two. Very small ones, as the duchess said."

"Before too late?"

"I'm thirty-nine."

"What about Inspector Dalgliesh?"

"Who?"

"Your policeman."

"He's a sergeant. I don't know. I've no idea what he thinks about that. You see," here she looked around, "you and I have gone a lot further in the last hour than I have with Brendan. Actually, the first question isn't about marriage, but about where we would live."

"But you are already established, aren't you? You have a practice. Where?"

"In Newbury. About six hundred miles west of here."

"My. What a country this is. You realize that's as far away as Edinburgh if you live where I do? And he's in the local— what? Detachment? Of the what? O.P.P.? Oh, I see. Like the army. He could get posted. And you'd have to follow. But you have a practice in Newbury. I see. At home sometimes people do live and love at a distance, even after they get married. All the ones who work for oil companies. They get together at weekends. But with you it could involve planes. Might be a bit of a stretch. I'll give it a bit of thought, but I doubt if I will come up with anything. It's a very Canadian problem, isn't it? All these distances. Still, you've taken my mind off Susan and my son-in-law, for which relief, much thanks."

Simon said, "When my grandfather died, my father gave me the job of going through his papers. It wasn't a very big job: Granddad was a schoolteacher in Moose Jaw, Saskatchewan. When he retired they moved to Loon Lake to be near my father, who had a parish there by then. They had led a fairly quiet life. Just one trip out of the country to Falkirk in

Scotland, where his father had emigrated from. A lot of old country people do that, don't they, try to uncover their roots, so to speak? Never mind all that, though; I wanted to tell you about my grandfather, the writer. First, among these papers was an attempt to write up the family history, perhaps inspired by his trip to Scotland. But some of the other writings were obviously attempts at telling stories, fiction, and some of them were even professionally typed—you know, nicely set up on the page, no errors—you could tell."

"Were they any good?"

"You mean as stories, something someone outside the family would be interested in? I don't think so. They were nearly all sort of built around a major irony. It was the taste of the times, I would think, but he didn't catch it very well. At any rate, there was no sign that he had got anything printed in a magazine, nothing like that."

"What are you doing?"

"There was an ant on your bottom. Gone now. I'll pick the next one off with my teeth."

"I'll look forward to that. Good. That it? For Granddad, the writer, I mean?"

"There was one story that was different from the rest. It wasn't professionally typed and yet was much more full of life than anything else. It was about when he was a student at the university. He had to earn the money for his board and room and fees, just as hard then as now, but he got lucky. It was the time of the Leduc oilfield discovery and for three years this construction company in Winnipeg sent him out every spring to look after the field office of their crew, making up the payroll and keeping track of the supplies. The money was very good, and apparently it came with free board and room.

"One year he met a boy on the bus going west, and they travelled side by side unspeaking all day until, well into the night, in a diner somewhere, a bus stop in the middle of the prairies, they started to talk. Afterwards, he wrote, he should have recognized that the boy was dying to talk, and as soon as the boy started to, he did recognize it. It was pretty clear,

Granddad said, that the boy, who was maybe a year or two younger than Granddad, had something on his mind, and then it was pretty clear what it was, because he wanted to know if Granddad had a girlfriend, ever enjoyed her, so to speak; in a series of 'did you ever—have you ever…' beginnings, it became clear that the boy wanted to share his experience. Granddad didn't have any experience to share (this was 1948) but he could tell that this was all about sharing so he pretended he did, intimated more than said anything, and then listened while the boy told his story.

"He was Swedish—from a Swedish immigrant family, that is—and he had boarded the bus at the little town of Stockholm to ride to Edmonton, where he had a job waiting as one of the workers who loaded *The Edmonton Journal* onto the delivery trucks at night. His brother had got him the job and later in the night, somewhere in the middle of Alberta, the boy offered to ask his brother, when they got to Edmonton, if he should try to get my Granddad a job. Granddad thanked him, said he had a job, but let the boy tell his story.

"The night before the boy left Stockholm, the town threw a party for him. Apparently a young man leaving the community was an event and they always had a farewell party for him at the community centre. The men mostly had mickeys of rye whiskey, which they tried to persuade the girls to drink—you know the sort of thing. And then someone announced that the boy had just got engaged to his girl, "to make sure she stayed put until I get back," and everyone cheered. And then, at the end, he took the girl home, and left her at the door. A little while later he shinnied up the drainpipe and let himself in through the lighted open window. And that was that.

"It wasn't, though, because the boy wanted to know if Granddad had had the same experience. It was, he said, the first time for him and the greatest thing that had ever happened to him. He said he and his girl had often talked about it, and agreed to wait, but they had waited long enough. He stayed with her until the sun came up, then he left down the same drainpipe, collected his bag from his house, and went down to the highway to wait for the bus. He didn't want to see or talk to anyone; now he was going to the city and as soon as he saved enough money he was going to find a room for both of them and he would go back and marry her and she would come to Edmonton, and they'd be together. But the thing he wanted to share was how good it was, that night. Was it like that for Granddad? Granddad lied, and said that it was, then he had to pretend to fall asleep, because the boy wanted to compare every detail of the experience.

"Of course, Granddad wrote, he couldn't make a story out of it. It was just what happened on the road to Edmonton."

Millie said, "I can see why the story should come up now."

"Yes. That story came back, the whole story came back, here, on the shore of this lake, just now."

Millie reached for a towel and sat up. "Simon," she said. "I have to tell you; I love you very much. You've always reminded me of Laurence Olivier when he played Hamlet in that movie, you know with the blond hair and all. I think you're incredibly lovely and I want to eat you up and I'm glad it is so—well, so good between us at last, but I think you—we—should move on, talk about where we should live, what you like for breakfast, things like that."

He said, "Oh, I know. This was all about me, as they say." He laughed loudly. "But it changes you, doesn't it? Do you feel it?"

She turned around and put on her shirt. "Let's go for a paddle," she said.

George Slocombe appeared, red-faced, sweaty, breathless. "They let me play," he said. He wore brown trainers and black Madras shorts and had hung a handkerchief from the back of his cap to protect his neck.

"Baseball? You don't know how. Do you, George? A hidden talent? Another one like your tango on the cruise last year?"

"They don't call it baseball in Canada," George said. "It's softball. They throw the ball underarm—I think so that the girls can play."

Winnie said, "They play baseball—hardball and softball. There are male softball leagues. There's a team in Newbury, sponsored by Harvey's Sporting Goods."

"Really?" Slocombe said, adding, "Well, we have women playing cricket. Christ, I'm hot." His neckerchief was limp with sweat. He tugged it off to wipe his face.

"Go for a swim," Sarah suggested.

"Did you bring my swim trunks?" Slocombe asked rhetorically.

One of the camp workers who had assisted in the shore lunch, and was sitting in the shade of a rock, smoking, said, "Go round the point. No one'll see you."

"I haven't got a towel," Slocombe pointed out.

Winnie called, "Here" and threw him one she took from her shoulder bag. "It belongs to the lodge. I brought it to sit on. I won't need it now."

Slocombe looked from one amused, slightly taunting face to another. "No need for that," he said, accepting the challenge, "Not these days." He stood up and kicked off his trainers, slipped off his shirt and pants and stood up, as if to the manner born, in his Y-fronts.

"George!" Sarah called, but not very firmly. "George!" more loudly as he fumbled with the waistband of his shorts. "Remember the children."

"And me," Winnie called. "Remember me."

Slocombe extended his waistband, let it snap back, then walked firmly down to the dock and dived into the lake, actually *onto* the lake in a perfect belly-flop, surfaced immediately and thrashed out a few yards before he paused and turned to wave.

Sarah said, "He was like this on the cruise. If he takes his shorts off and starts waving it about, read your book."

Slocombe waded noisily ashore and picked up the towel. "Arrugh," he bellowed.

"Ruuaagh."

"I hear you've been swimming," his wife said. "Stand over there if you're going to shake your hair about."

George finished the display of his ablutions and sat down next to Winnie.

She asked, "What game would you usually play on the sand in England, George? When you go to the seaside?"

"If we still go to the seaside. Nobody I know still does. Still, cricket," George said. "If you were well-organized you'd have a mat to roll out so you could bowl."

"Are you a good batter, George?"

"Batsman," he corrected her. "I was once. And I mean once. One day when I was thirteen."

"George!" Sarah said. "Winnie doesn't want to hear about your adolescent exploits."

"Yes, she does," Winnie said. "Hit well that day, did you, George?"

"Batted," Slocombe said. "Make yourself comfortable. I'll tell you about it." He put himself on stage, waited for them to become an audience, and told them his oft-told tale of the day he got the power, the day he could have batted for England:

"I liked cricket and I worked very hard in my pre-teen years to make myself useful. I learned to bowl an off-break, but then I couldn't bowl anything else, not even a straight ball, and the batsmen soon learned this and knocked me about. As a batsman, I learned early that if I was anything, I was a swiper; that is, the only stroke that came naturally to me was the drive to square leg, the swipe. To do this, whatever the kind of ball being delivered, I stepped smartly to the right, swung the bat as in baseball and swiped the ball, often to the boundary for four runs." Slocombe demonstrated, using an imaginary bat. "This seemed to me a natural stroke. Sometimes it worked, but mostly it didn't.

"On this day it worked every time. On the afternoon set aside for games' practice I found myself at bat, facing the bowling of a boy named Knox (not his real name). We were being supervised by a science teacher named Baker (not his name, either) who by his accent, and his clothes—ancient and scruffy—showed that in teaching us he had come down a class or two. Baker, this teacher, even wore a pair of old cricket boots, yellow from age but the real thing. They symbolized his attitude to the afternoon's exercise: although he did not plan to show us how it was done but to tell us, the wearing of the boots showed what he thought was important.

"'Now, keep a straight bat, Slocombe', he called.

"Even at thirteen I knew that was a metaphor from the world of Baker's boyhood. It meant, 'Face up to life, die if you must but put your best foot forward in the meantime and stop picking your nose, lying, and masturbating'."

"George!" Sarah protested automatically.

Slocombe ignored her.

"But on the cricket pitch it still meant just what it said.

"Now Knox, the bowler, came from the same caste as the master. Unlike the rest of us, he and two others had not won scholarships to get them out of the tenements of inner London, but actually paid fees. The rest of us brought our mostly humble origins with us to the grammar school, our accents, our eating habits, and clothes that reflected that we got a grant from the council to buy the school uniform at the same official supplier. But Knox (and two others) had fathers who wore ties to work and Knox's clothes had been bought at one of the big stores in the West End probably, not Harrods, perhaps, but Dickens & Jones, at least. So his jacket was a slightly darker, more olive shade of green than ours, and his grey flannel shorts and later his first long trousers were charcoal-coloured and smooth, and his shoes were not shod with metal studs to make them last. The other details, the hair cut slightly longer than ours (no 'short back and sides, please' for him), the pocket handkerchief, the real leather satchel, the Parker pen and pencil set, all confirmed his status; he was probably at our school because his father had applied too late to get him into a public school, he, his father (a colonial administrator, no doubt) having returned to England unexpectedly, because of the war perhaps, or perhaps suddenly impoverished (but with enough money left for the good clothes). It wasn't Knox's fault; he made no effort to assert his social superiority but he was unable to conceal his origins. Not quite a loner, but prevented by his superior accent from bonding with any of the little gangs in the class, he acquired an acolyte as such people always do, at school and later, a toady, someone who had no friends among the rest of us and looked only to serve Knox, thus confirming Knox's status.

"So Knox was to bowl and I was to bat. When I was bowled out, within two or three balls no doubt, the next boy would come up for batting practice and some other boy would get a chance to practice his bowling.

"I watched Knox and Mr. Baker exchange companionate remarks as I waited for the first ball. Although Mr. Baker was of Knox's class, as a schoolmaster he had become impoverished. It was evident, though it is hard to say why, that his clothes had once come from the same clothier as Knox's. The tweed jacket must have been twenty years old but this was a time when it was acceptable for impoverished schoolmasters to sew leather patches on the elbows of old jackets. Knox and Mr. Baker had similar accents, not the bleating noises of the leaders of the Conservative party but the accents I came later to associate with that portion of the middle class that worked for a living, colonial administrators and naval officers, for example.

"Now Mr. Baker turned towards me as Knox paced out the five or six steps of his run-up to the wicket. He cleared his face, as one would clear one's throat, of the agreeableness that talking to Knox had put there. He looked at me as he framed the corrective remark he knew would be necessary in talking to my kind (I don't mean to imply that Mr. Baker was harsh, or bullying, or spiteful, or otherwise wicked in his relationships with his pupils; no, he just had found it always necessary with my kind, the nose-pickers, to begin, in class, with something like, 'Sit up straight, boy. Now...' which he never needed with Knox).

"'Now', he said, 'Put your feet in the proper position; bend your elbow and (again) keep a straight bat'! He turned to Knox, smiled and nodded for him to begin bowling.

"Knox trotted up to the wicket at his end, signalling by the shortness of his run and the general lack of agitation about his upper body as he brought his arm round and over that he was not going to bowl fast, but might spin the ball to make it break as he had been trained to do at some other school by a better-dressed full-time games master. I, on the other hand, had had no formal instruction at all; I just knocked a cricket ball about on Tuesday afternoons with thirty or forty other boys.

"So the ball came at me down the centre of the wicket, pitched to bounce a couple of feet in front of me, where I could either step forward and smother it, sending it back to Knox, or step back and strike it properly, perhaps trying for an elegant shot to mid-off, or even trying for a late cut as it went past, sending it through the slips, though such a stroke was well beyond me.

"The first ball bounced neatly in front of me, a well-delivered ball for me to stroke back to Knox, though usually when I tried this perfectly simple (and classical) shot, the ball nicked the edge of my bat and spun into the waiting hands of one of the fielders. Or I missed it completely and it struck me in the crotch and everyone laughed and I was given 'Out'! by Mr. Baker, 'Leg Before Wicket'.

"I had no intention of playing by their rules, which enough experience had shown didn't work for me, so I jumped at the first ball and smothered it with my bat before it could hurt me and when I stepped back it lay dead in the grass.

"'Keep a straight bat, Slocombe', Mr. Baker called, looking irritated.

"But I had seen something I had never seen before. Fifty years later I read that the great baseball hitter, Ted Williams, could see the baseball he was going to hit so clearly that he could read the name of the manufacturer. I would never have believed it, except that on that day I saw the cricket ball in the same way—big, slow, easy to hit. The next ball came down along the same path and bounced in the same place. As it bounced, I stepped smartly to the right and hit it over the heads of the fielders on my left, hit it with a baseball stroke, hit it with open shoulders and so much follow-through I nearly went right round in a circle.

"'Keep a straight bat', Mr. Baker shouted, angry now. This wasn't cricket.

"The next ball unbelievably came along the same trajectory, and again I hit it for four. Knox was clearly as limited in his choice of balls as I was in my choice of strokes; he had no breaking balls in his armoury, and his single weapon—the ball bowled correctly at my middle stump—was a much severer limitation on him than my single stroke, the swipe to leg, was on me.

"Knox bowled three more and I sent them all to the boundary. The master called a halt and came down the pitch to speak to me. 'Now', he said, demonstrating a proper stance in front of the wicket. 'Bowl, Knox'.

"Knox trotted forward and sent one of his correct deliveries down the pitch; the master took a step forward and stroked the ball smoothly and elegantly back to him. 'See'? he asked me. He repeated the stroke to show me how his body produced it, the shoulder pointed forward and lined up with the left knee, the parts finely articulated. 'A straight bat'. He walked back to the far wicket. I took my stance, my hands, feet, shoulder and left knee correctly linked. Knox began his run, released the ball, and I stepped to the right and clouted it to the boundary.

"The master was very angry. Knox just looked unhappy—I learned to like him later, in the fifth form, when my accent had improved—and waited for further instructions. Then he and Mr. Baker put their heads together.

"They were obviously planning strategy, a strategy that I assumed would succeed, because I had no counter-strategy of my own. I just had the power, temporarily, and I didn't even know then that's what it was. All I could do was give myself over to it. I had no thought of preparing myself should Knox try to attack my batting with something other than slow balls sent down the middle. As it turned out, the power that day was greater than I knew, greater than Knox's ability to thwart it. The next ball came down at the same speed as ever but pitched slightly farther away on the right. The proper response would have been a smart stroke through mid-off but I just had my swipe-to-leg so I leaped a yard to the right to get into my position, three or four feet away from the stumps, and then swiped the ball to the leg boundary.

"Knox looked appealingly at Mr. Baker. Again, this wasn't cricket. The master muttered something, his face dark, and Knox sent down another ball, this time a further foot away, more than a yard away from me, so far away it would have to have broken through a right angle to affect me, and Knox didn't bowl breaks like that so I ignored it as it sailed harmlessly past.

"And so it went for the rest of the afternoon. Whenever the ball came near me I hit it to the square leg boundary. I was never tempted to chase the balls that Knox sent very wide on either side. By now I had a cheering section. All the other practice games on the field had ended as the entire school stopped to watch what they assumed to be a duel between me and Knox. I didn't like this: just as the gods had favoured me that day with the power, so instinct said they would equally punish any show of pride, any indication on my part that I might claim the credit for what I was doing, and I tried continually to show by my demeanor that this was a 'friendly' contest, smiling a lot, and making head-shaking signs of approval at anything like a near miss on Knox's part. Even though I hadn't Knox's background, I knew how to behave.

"Many of the other boys had already been infected by the 'play-up-and-play-the-game' spirit represented by Mr. Baker, and they cheered every time I seemed to have any difficulty. One or two of them began sucking up to Mr. Baker by calling out insulting remarks, directed at me. 'What do you think this is—Rounders'? one shouted. It was a weak shot, though, because whatever I was doing it wasn't in any way the act of a panty-waist. Much closer to scoring a wound was the shout, 'Where did you learn to bat, Slocombe? Borstal'?

"Borstal was the name of the reformatory schools for delinquent boys.

"I ignored them all, as did Knox and Mr. Baker. This was a struggle that concerned us three only.

"My own cronies cheered my every swipe, including in their encouragement a slogan, mocking the values of the other side: 'No matter how you play the game, it's win or lose that counts', they called.

"The afternoon came to an end at four-thirty, and I retired undefeated. My claque wanted to chair me off the field, but I thought that might give Mr. Baker a stroke, and I didn't want to sadden Knox any further, either. In fact I trotted down the pitch to shake hands and keep the gods at bay, and it is a tribute to his background and training that Knox accepted my hand briefly before jumping onto his bike and pedalling off with his toady. I didn't blame him. Even his bike was a new Raleigh with a Sturmey-Archer three-speed gear, and he had been defeated by someone with a secondhand machine whose tires didn't match.

"What happened next was a let-down, as it was bound to be. A week later we assembled again for cricket practice. Mr. Baker said, harshly, to me 'Take the bat, Slocombe', and to Knox, 'You will begin the bowling'.

"Knox assumed a stiff upper lip and turned to begin his run. Afterwards Baker was reported as saying, in the masters' common room, 'I don't know what happened the week before. We've all had the experience of seeing someone unlikely do something extraordinary once. But it is always a fluke. What we saw was an afternoon-long fluke, and I felt I had a duty the following week to show that that's what it was. I don't pretend to understand it all, but I did feel it wouldn't happen again'.

"He was right. Knox pitched his first ball, slightly short, accidentally, I'm sure, and harder than usual so it arrived at the wicket shoulder-high and fast and I didn't know what to do with it. I just managed to avoid it.

"Knox and Mr. Baker exchanged glances, as they say, and Knox came back with another. Not immediately, actually. It took him three more balls to get close to his first and when he found the mark the second time I was lucky to see the ball sail over the wicket. The third time he got everything right and I was out. I simply wasn't sure whether to run forward and try to hit it as a full toss before it bounced, or stand back a bit and catch it after it bounced. I didn't have the power any longer and my indecision meant that I managed to hit the ball but only with the end of the bat, sending it looping up and down straight into the safe hands of Knox.

"'Well done, Knox', Baker said, and then, so happy was he, to me, 'Don't lean back, Slocombe, when you are playing the ball forward. Get over the top of it. Well done, though. You did well last week'.

"But I wasn't listening; I was shaking hands with Knox in mid-pitch, beginning our friendship."

Winnie said, "You've told that story before, George."

"He's been telling that bloody story for twenty years," Sarah Slocombe said. "Ever since it went over well at an office outing."

George said, "I've polished it, though, over the years, and significantly changed the sub-text, haven't I, Sarah? Isn't that what the people in the *Guardian* call it? The sub-text? I read about it somewhere, changed it to a tale of how an angry lower-class young scholarship boy rose to be a man of means. Made some money; went up the scale. You know. When I had made a few bob, people like Baker and Knox didn't bother me. Actually I liked Knox when I met him later. Just shows you."

"And the science teacher, Mr. Baker?"

"Oh, no. He was hopeless. I thought about him a lot. He was an idealist who believed in the whole class, know-your-place thing. Harmless unless he's in charge."

"But you don't. Believe in it."

"I wish I did. It's like believing in God. Allows you to think it's not all your fault."

At the wheel of the pontoon, the pilot was talking on his cell phone. He hung up and called to his mate in the front to come back. "Problems," he said, not loudly enough to be heard by any of the guests. "They don't want us back too early."

The pilot and his mate exchanged monosyllables, came to an agreement, and the pilot cleared his throat. "Ladies and gentlemen," he said in a hoarse parody of a white tour guide's voice, "'Case anyone is wondering, we missed out on that rain and I'm taking us home a different way so you can see the whole country. It'll take a bit longer but it's a nice ride, so put your feet up and enjoy the scenery."

"Do you mind if I sit here? Eva Sheridan."

Eva Sheridan was a small woman in her mid-sixties with carefully set hair and rimless glasses. She was carrying a new-looking book. She had been at their table the night before, sitting more or less silently beside Winnie during the early banter. Then, when Donner had exploded his small grenade, Winnie noticed that Eva Sheridan had failed to be outraged. In fact, she had giggled a little in an accommodating way, as if wanting to be one of the party, even if things were getting a bit vulgar. Or perhaps Eva was earthier than she looked.

Now Winnie said, "What did you think of Mr Donner's contribution to Mrs. Hepburn's tale of twins? I thought he might be a minister, but not when he said that."

"I thought it was funny," Eva Sheridan said.

And still do, thought Winnie, judging by the expression on your face. "Tell me," she said. "What made you come to Dempsey's Lodge?" It was slightly rude, but legitimate. Dempsey's Lodge had had to become all things to all people in order to survive, but even so, Eva Sheridan's sky-blue pantsuit seemed slightly out of place.

"I'm on a pilgrimage," Eva said. "My brother worked here once, for a summer. It is one of the few things I know about his life in the last sixty years, so I thought I'd make the trip, see if anyone remembered him."

"And have you found anyone?"

"There's no one left from then. Even the old man who lives in that little house along the shore doesn't remember him, probably because Eddie was here before him."

"A wasted trip, then?"

"Oh, no. No way. I told you, a pilgrimage. I wanted to see if I could learn a bit more about my brother by coming here. I haven't learned anything about his life here, but I think I've found out there's nothing more to learn, so my pilgrimage has turned into, well, a pilgrimage."

George Slocombe approached. "Did you notice the accent of the bloke who made the rude remark last night?" he asked. "Perhaps a Canadian wouldn't hear it. He was a toff. Only a toff would get away with that. If I'd said that word everyone would know it was my lower-class origins showing."

"Give it a rest, George," Sarah Slocombe said, from her seat by the other rail. "There are no toffs in Canada."

Slocombe looked slightly confused, but not unhappy.

Winnie said to Eva, once Slocombe had wandered away. "What happened to your brother?"

"He died."

"Recently? How long since you'd seen him?"

"Sixty years. But we were very close as kids, and when I heard he was dying I left for Toronto right away. I knew there must be things to be done, arrangements to be made. Besides…"

Winnie recognized that Eva was off now, and settled back for a story.

"How old was your brother when he left Brandon?" she asked.

"Fifteen. He didn't leave; he was kicked out by our father, or maybe he ran away to escape him. Father banned discussion of the boy in his own lifetime, simply announcing one day at supper that Eddie was gone, and we were not to refer to him again. 'His type's not wanted around here', Father said, and that was that. If anyone outside the house inquired, we were to say that the boy had run off, no one knew where. It was the answer that would end the questions soonest. 'We don't know', we were told to say. You sure I'm not keeping you from something?"

"No, no, no. Tell me about your brother."

"Where was I?"

"Your brother was dying in Toronto."

"All right, then. Well, Margaret and our other third sister, Katie, speculated about what Eddie could have done that justified banishment (I was too young for such talk); stealing something, for instance, would have meant just a whipping. They agreed in the end that it must have been something wicked, something boys do, but there they were stuck. Margaret told me later when she visited Father in the nursing home before he died that he was muttering about a "filthy swine" whom he had become obsessed with in his senility. He could only mean Eddie, unmentioned for forty years. But the actual rumours had already dried up; only the memory that there had been whispers stayed."

Winnie said, "Where was your mother at the time?"

"She died when I was three. I was raised by my sisters. They were good to me, but I think we missed a lot, especially as children. Our father was a bit strict, doing his duty, but not given much to games and such. We had no dependents, and so we were entitled to some fun in our old age. Lately, now we've found out how safe travel in a group can be, we've joined tours that have taken us as far as Italy and Greece."

"Greece!" Mrs Hepburn called from across the deck. "Did I hear Greece? I love Greece, though I've only been to Corfu and Lefkada for a week each, and never to Athens."

"On tours?" Winnie asked her, politely.

"Of course. I'm still an object of interest to Mediterranean men so I feel safe in a tour group. And there's someone to talk to…"

"Have you seen much of the rest of Europe?" Winnie cut in. She would have to wait for a suitable opportunity to get rid of Mrs. Hepburn, she decided, and hear the rest of Eva's story; in the meantime it seemed possible to make Mrs. Hepburn's presence useful. Winnie had never travelled abroad, anywhere. She had missed doing the usual student travels for lack of money and had been concentrating on her practice ever since graduation. She had taken comfort once at a reading given by her favourite Canadian writer, who had remarked simply, but astonishingly, in answer to a question from the audience, that she had never been to Europe. And yet she was a wonderful writer. That had calmed Winnie down, made her realize that she should listen only to herself in making her choices. To listen, as another favourite writer had said once, to her heart. But when she did that, she still wanted to pack and go, desire turning into a need, a need to find out what she was missing.

Eva's voice cut in sharply, her tone harsh, before Winnie could speak. "Give us a minute, will you, missus? I'm in the middle of a story. You can have your turn after." She fixed Mrs. Hepburn with a glittering eye until the other woman backed off.

"Sorry," Mrs. Hepburn said. "Sorry, sorry, sorry, sorry. I'll come back later, shall I?"

"Eddie died before the train reached Toronto," Eva continued, after Mrs. Hepburn left. "I had a room booked at the Journey's End on Church Street, and as soon as I freshened up I went directly on to Eddie's lawyer, who was waiting for me in his office. Fred Butcher, his name was. He turned out all right. He was a very tall, soft-spoken man who wore bright suspenders like a country lawyer in an old movie, sort of Gary Cooperish.

"'I didn't know your brother well', he began.

"I interrupted. 'But what *did* you know? He wasn't a criminal or anything, was he'?

"'No, no. Er, he never married, did you know that'?

"I said, 'What does that mean in Toronto, Mr. Butcher'?

"He stopped me, holding up his hand. 'Let me get on. I'll tell you what I know about his life, and you'll see. He bought a house a long time ago in an area called Deer Park. Do you know Toronto? No. Well, when he bought the house, Deer Park was just midtown Toronto, but since then it's become— desirable. He paid seventeen thousand for the house in 1960. I think it's probably worth thirty times that now. Of course he did a lot of work on it'.

"'Where did *he* work'?

"'For the last fifty years he was a clerk in a hardware store. Before that he had some part-time jobs. When he first left home, he worked at a fishing camp. He got his board and room free there, so he was able to save some to come to Toronto in the fall when the camp closed up'."

Eva paused and commented on the story. "That fishing camp would be here, Dempsey's Lodge. I came across some photos later on when I went to Eddie's house, and one had the front of the lodge with the name. So I thought I'd come up here, have a look. But, as I said, no one remembers him. Let me get on. So I asked the lawyer now, 'Did he leave anything, apart from the house'?

"The lawyer nodded. 'Would you like me to look after the estate'?

"'I'd been steeling myself with a question. 'What's your fee, Mr. Butcher'?

"He smiled. He was a really nice man. 'About two thousand dollars'.

"'That was about what I'd been told to expect. 'What else'? I asked now.

"'He had a couple of savings bonds and a bit in the bank. About twenty thousand dollars. That all comes to you two. You can pay me when you get it, or I'll deduct my fee from the final settlement, if you want me to handle it'.

"I nodded. 'That's very fair. What about the house? And didn't he have a car'?

"'No car. He wouldn't drive after his accident. Let me read you the will. It's very short'. He mumbled rapidly until he came to the bequests. 'And I bequeath my house to Miss Janet Howe...'

"'Who'?

"'Miss Janet Howe'.

"I waited for an explanation.

"'She was a friend of his for many years, I understand. As much as thirty, maybe more'. He looked down at the will '… in appreciation of the many good years she has given me', he read.

"The two of us looked at each other. It was as if the lawyer was one of the family. I spoke up, 'A *lady* friend'?

"He nodded.

"'That answers *that* question', I said. 'Can I meet her'?

"'I'm afraid not. I've been in touch with her. She has asked me to sell the house and deposit the money in a new account for her, and act as her agent. She lives with her mother. I'm just guessing, but I think her mother doesn't know about her relationship with your brother'.

"'How old is she? Her, not her mother. Her mother must be about a hundred'.

"Baker considered the question. 'They were of an age', he said, finally. 'Your brother and her'.

"'Then you won't find us contesting', I said. 'She's entitled. They were…a couple. She did a lot more for him than we did, even though that's not our fault'.

"'Good', the lawyer said. 'Are there any other relatives? The will just says the estate is to be shared equally among his sisters. Nothing about anyone else'.

"'No. That's it, then'? I asked.

"'He left the contents of the house to you, too'.

"'Holy cow! What on earth for? People usually leave house and contents together, don't they? They do in Brandon'.

"He thumbed his suspenders. 'I think he thought that might be awkward for her'.

"'Right. She couldn't take them home to Mum, could she'? That made him laugh. 'A lover'. I said. 'I wonder what she's like'?

"'Now', he said, 'tell me what you know about Eddie. Why do you think he left home'?

"I came close, then, to telling him the truth but I held back. There was no way to tell it that wouldn't reflect badly on Eddie, and it wouldn't be fair to Margaret after all this time of her not knowing. And he might wonder if I was making it up. Besides, I still didn't feel that I knew it all. What I did remember was dozing on a warm summer afternoon in the bedroom of a farmhouse on the prairies and Eddie kneeling beside the bed, kissing my cheek and saying words that were lost in the noise our father was making. And that was that, until later."

"What's the matter?" Mrs. Hepburn called.

"We're turning round," Winnie said.

The pontoon was in the middle of a small lake, turning slowly to face its own wake. "We must be on our way back."

The Slocombes were moving down the rail towards them, evidently wanting to chat. Winnie shook her head at them, a bit rudely, trying to imply by gestures and her facial expression that she was looking after a distressed Eva. She could explain later. Right now she wanted to hear the end of Eva's story.

"What happened then?" she asked.

"Give me a minute," Eva said. She blew her nose. "I spent one more night in the motel so as to go up the CN Tower and buy some little mementoes to take back to the ladies in our bridge club. Then I decided to come up to Dempsey's Lodge, as I said, just in case it would help to fill in one more gap in the story of Eddie's life. I thought of it as a sort of personal memorial. I knew the word for what had happened, the fashionable term, even in Brandon: closure. At last I could put Eddie away."

"Am I still interrupting?" It was Mrs. Hepburn, hovering.

"No, no..." Winnie responded.

Eva cut her off. "Five more minutes," she said, harshly, eye glittering. "I'm nearly there." Then, to herself, "Woman's a bloody nuisance."

She turned back to Winnie, urgent with the need to finish her story. "For fifty years I had spent some part of every day

81

wondering what had happened to him. Winnipeg, Toronto—these were big places for a young boy, and we had had no news of him. Margaret and I had agreed that it was possible that he was still alive, but that was all. There was a man we knew in Brandon whose father used to tell a story about the depression days in Toronto, about a young lad who used to stand on the corner of Yonge Street and Dundas, and recite that poem 'The Ancient Mariner' all the way through. He had it memorized and he recited it as if he was playing a violin, for spare change. This man, the man in Brandon who told me the story—he was a baker by trade—was so impressed that years later, when he retired, he took a course in poetry that included 'The Ancient Mariner' just so he could find out a bit about it. I always connected his story of the boy reciting 'The Ancient Mariner' to get some eating money, begging, with my memory of Eddie. But let me get on.

"As we grew up past the age Eddie was when he had left, he stayed fifteen in my mind. As I say, in my mind he became a young boy, then a waif, Oliver Twist, a street-person on Toronto's Yonge Street, and, as I say, I connected him with the baker's story. But when I heard the truth, it didn't surprise me that he had led such a quiet and regular existence after all, saving his money, buying a house, trying to make a home, accumulating all the furnishings, although without trying to put them in order. Leaving the house to his girlfriend meant that that side of his life must have been good enough, too. I didn't have to mourn for him anymore. See, there was one more bit I should have mentioned. Among the other stuff Lionel found in the bureau was a bundle of Christmas cards, real old ones, with messages like, 'Merry Xmas, Eddie, from Mr. and Mrs. Driver at Number 66'. Now the thing was, that Christmas he was already working at the hardware store. When I put that together with the Christmas cards I decided he must have had two jobs, one of them probably to do with delivering newspapers or some such. At his age, I thought that was pretty gutsy, and I stopped feeling sad about him. I just had to take a little trip up here in case he was still remembered, but I had his story pretty straight already. So that was all right. It was all coming together, I felt, though I wasn't sure what 'it' was. The final bit would come together when I remembered the words that Eddie had said as he knelt beside the bed, and then, as I tried one more time to bring his words back, I found the answer in some words he must have meant. I didn't actually remember the words but I knew what must have happened, what the words must have been. See, that afternoon he found me I was his sleeping beauty, and he woke me up with a kiss. I hope it stayed with him. It did with me. It's easy to tell you all this, because I'll never see you again, will I?

"The next day, I was to take the train back to Winnipeg, but I stopped off here. I didn't really expect to hear any more news of Eddie, but now I can imagine his whole life from the time he left home. As I said, I've been on a pilgrimage. Thank you for listening to me. It was nice to have someone to talk to, get the story straight before I decide what to tell them back in Brandon."

"The ladies you play bridge with? You'll tell them all about the sleeping beauty?"

Eva considered this. "No," she said. "I don't believe I will. I'll tell them I came here to see if there was any news of Eddie, but there wasn't any. There was, though, wasn't there?"

Winnie said, "I'm not sure I'm getting this."

Eva said, "He was my brother. That's not in the old story, is it, the original one? I know I might sound obsessed, but everybody's a psychologist nowadays, and I don't want that bridge group analysing me. And then there's Father. What was his problem? We'll never know, will we, but that won't stop the bridge group speculating," she ended, again fixing Winnie with an eye as she did so.

Winnie, after a very long pause in which she wondered if the old lady was truly mad, said, "Now, let's ask the boatman if there's any beer left over from lunch. Your story's made me thirsty."

Simon said, "I wonder if Adam felt—well—stressed, before he ate the apple."

"What are you talking about now, Simon?"

"You know, the Book of Genesis. The whole story of Adam and Eve and the snake and the apple. It was all there, this morning, up on that rock."

"Was it?"

"Yes. We were in the Garden before, now we are in the wilderness."

She looked around her at the Northern Ontario scene of silver birch, rocky shoreline, sparkling water and blue sky. "I suppose that's what you, being literary, could call it. Nice, though, isn't it?"

"Yes, it is. In Genesis it all turns to rat shit. I think it starts to rain. But nothing like that is happening to us."

"Not even allegorically."

"No. 'Into her dream he melted'."

"This is Adam still?"

"No. Keats. Can I say one more thing?"

"If you have to."

"Lawrence was right. Have you read *Sons and Lovers*?"

"Of course I have. Now let's step back into the wilderness. It's starting to rain again, have you noticed? And what do you think that smoke is over there?"

"There's that plane again, the Lands and Forests one," Bert Tyrell said. "They must be looking for something."

The sky was threatening again and it was time to think of going home.

"I don't know what they call themselves now, but the Department of Lands and Forests was renamed about thirty years ago," Brendan Copps said.

"You know who I mean, the people that worry about the wildlife. 'Ullo! Look over there. Whassat? Smoke. Over there.

It's coming from the camp. Someone burning rubbish? You 'ad enough fishing? I 'ave. Let's go in and have a look." He turned the motor up and swung the boat around. "And it's more than a bit of rubbish, mate. One of the cabins is on fire. That's what that plane was all about."

"Let's go, then. Thank God for the picnic. Chances are there won't be anyone involved."

"It's one of the cabins, all right. When we get over there I won't bother with the dock, just run us up on the beach. Be faster. Okay?"

"Christ, look at it go. Who's that on the road?"

"Marcel and Ted Revell. Couple of the workers who didn't go into town. They're trying to get the equipment on the fire trolley going."

"That's the fire trolley?"

"A pump and a hundred feet of hose is what it carries. Now, Brendan, old son, jump!"

"God Almighty." Deborah Wilkie sat up to look out the window. "We're on fire. Look!"

Lenny Kollberg hauled himself upright and stared through the glass. He reached for his clothes, scrambling to get out. "You stay here," he said.

"Until someone comes for me with a cup of tea? I'm in your bed, remember?" She pulled her clothes into a pile in front of her as she thought about her situation. "Make sure there's no one in the lounge," she said, when she was ready. "I'll go out there, wait a couple of minutes, then scream. Okay?"

"Why?"

"BECAUSE I WILL BE LOOKING OUT THE WINDOW AND SEEING THE BLOODY FIRE. Now, look out the door. Anyone around? Now go!"

Brendan Copps leaped from the boat and ran up the beach to the road and on to the burning cabin, where he took the hose from a struggling Marcel. Bert Tyrell followed more slowly.

"This it?" Copps asked Tyrell, pointing to the steady but quiet stream coming from the hose. "I could piss better than this. Can't we rev the pump up?"

"The answer is yes and no. Yes, this is all the fire-fighting equipment we've got, and no, that's a one-speed pump. I just finished repairing it. It's reliable but it doesn't have much oomph."

Just then the water slowed to a trickle. Bert Tyrell scuttled over to the generator, switched it off, switched it on, kicked it, took a kink out of the pipe, shook the pipe, and the water flowed again. "I'll stay here,"Tyrell said. "Don't touch a fucking thing, you guys."

"Tell those two..." Copps pointed to Marcel and Ted Revell, who were standing watching, "to beat out sparks, stop this spreading to the other cabins." He was shouting now as the flames roared.

Tyrell said, "I'll call the fire brigade in town." He took a mobile phone from his pocket and read the number off from the pump. "Trouble is, it's pretty much a volunteer crew and it'll take some time to get assembled and drive round the lake. As the others come in off the lake, get the adults to help keep the sparks from flying. But keep the kids away."

Lenny Kollberg appeared and ran towards them. "I was taking a nap," he said. "It looks like just one cabin has caught. We just have to keep it from spreading," he said. "Watch for sparks and keep pouring water on it. Thank God there's no wind. I'll get some buckets from the kitchen, start a bucket chain." He ran off to round up some helpers.

They watched the fire burn itself down for an hour before they could approach the blaze. The wood was pine, now eighty years old, and it did not take long for the fire to dispose of any fire-proofing the logs had ever received. By the time Kollberg returned with some buckets and a couple of assistant cooks to throw water on the embers, the worst was over. Kollberg said to one of the helpers, "We won't know for a long time that it won't flare up, so keep pouring water on it. And get a couple of rakes to go through the ashes."

Henry Hyacinth said to Kollberg, both of them watching the fire, "I took that guy Wilkie into town this morning. You know what he told me? He said he was going to tell you to get rid of me. That right?"

"No way he could do that, Henry. There's a group of lawyers in the city own this place. They want to build a casino here. They'll need guys like you. Especially while they build it."

"Wilkie seemed pretty sure."

Lenny Kollberg didn't like the sound of that, knowing from Deborah that Wilkie was a crook. He stared out at the lake. "I think he was bullshitting, letting you know what a big shot he is. But round here he is just a guest. A nobody."

"I don't think so. See, he was losing it with me, real pissed off he was, because I called him an asshole."

"Jesus, Henry, why did you do that? That doesn't help. He is a guest."

"That's what he is. A fucking asshole. Said it would take me five thousand years to catch up to him. I couldn't think of a good way to answer that, so I called him an asshole."

A crash and a shower of sparks.

"There goes the rest of the roof," Copps shouted. "Keep the water on the outside."

The sound of a fire truck came through the trees, then the truck itself, wailing the good news that it had arrived from the town.

Six volunteers in assorted dress jumped from the truck and swarmed round it, unreeling the hose to run it down to the dock and into the lake.

Brendan Copps said, "Wet the surrounding area down some more first. That bit of rain helped but it needs more."

"Who are you?" The driver of the truck and evidently the team leader asked Copps.

"One of the guests here."

"Then keep back, out of our way."

"Start the pump, Number One!" shouted the man on the dock.

The truck driver picked up the nozzle and shouted, "Switch on, Number Two."

The fireman by the truck said, "That's me," and leaned to the side of the truck and pushed a switch.

The nozzle leaped out of the fireman's grip and started snaking about the grass, soaking everyone in its way before Bert Tyrell acted to switch it off. The leader tried to recover his role. "Fred," he called to one of the other firemen, "Give me a hand. It takes two to hold this goddam thing."

With the hose tucked under the leader's arm, and two pairs of hands gripping the nozzle, the leader tried again. "Switch on!" he shouted. "Not full force yet."

"This is a one-speed pump," the other shouted back. "On or off?"

The two men took a firm grip. "Okay, but get ready to switch off," the leader shouted. This time they held it, and a forceful jet shot out, under control, and the leader began to issue a stream of instructions, to get closer and closer to the heart of the blaze until the force of the jet was starting to break up the last still-burning logs that had framed the cottage.

"Can't you control it at the nozzle?" One of the firemen by the truck called.

"We should've rehearsed this," the fireman holding the hose with the leader said.

"Switch off," called the leader.

With the water off, he read the words on the nozzle and twisted it to send a jet of a much bigger diameter but a quarter of the force, a perfect flow to flood the remaining fire. "Switch on," he shouted, looking around, sure of the response. "I can handle this on my own, George," he said to the other man on the hose. "You help out with the others."

They poured water on the smoking ruins for half an hour, then moved in with shovels and rakes to spread out the remaining embers. It was Bert Tyrell who noticed first that something among the embers looked odd. "Jesus wept," he said. "That's some poor bugger got caught. That's a body, for Chrissake."

The word ran round the assembly, now numbering about fifteen or twenty people including the firemen. All pressed forward to get a closer look.

"Who is it?" the fire chief asked of the crowd.

"That's what we need to find out," Copps said as he began to understand the situation, and realised that responding to it was his problem. He turned to the ring of onlookers who were pressing close to get a good look at the body. "Stay back," he called. "Right back. You," he said to the fire chief, "tell your guys to keep everyone back."

"This is a fire scene," the chief said. "I give the orders here."

"The fire's out," Copps said. "There's a body in there. My turn."

"And who are you, buddy, may I ask? One of the guests, right?"

Copps identified himself. Bert Tyrell, who had come up to the two men, said, "S'right. He is. Sergeant Copps of the Ontario Provincial Police." He offered a mock salute. "On holiday," he added.

The fireman sucked a tooth, absorbing this information. "In that case, the fire being out, I am supernumerary to this scene. Right? Okay, guys. Pack it up. May I know your name, Mister Policeman, so I can put in my report?"

Copps took a card from his wallet. "I'll call the local O.P.P. detachment," he said. "This isn't my territory. But I'll hold the place secure until they get here."

"That how you say it? 'Hold the place secure'?"

Copps thought he had never seen anyone so disgruntled as the fireman, his authority dissolving. Copps sought to reinforce it. "Chief, we have to cooperate until the local police get here," he said. "Ask your men to keep anyone from approaching. Post four of them around the site. You and I need a place away from the crowd to write up the incident."

"We'll use my truck," the fireman said, hearing now that he was being consulted as an equal, not ordered. "That way

I can supervise my team. My name's McCarthy, by the way. Harold McCarthy. Hal," he finally conceded.

"Brendan." He put out his hand, feeling he had successfully manoeuvred a tricky piece of water. "Brendan Copps."

"Over here, you guys," McCarthy called. "Now here is what I want you to do." He laid out the plan to block the site from the public, essentially assigning a man to each side of the smoking ruins.

Copps used the emergency number to speak to the inspector of the local detachment and tell him the story, but even as he dialled, an O.P.P. car wailed its way to a standstill beside him and two figures jumped out. "We got a call from the Natural Resources people. They'd sent a plane to see what the smoke was all about."

"Yeah, we saw the plane. Thought it was looking for the moose stranded up on the rock. What we've got here is a fire and a fatality," Copps said.

"I'm Inspector Rowan. You're who?"

"Sergeant Copps, Huronia detachment, here on holiday."

"So give me a quick verbal run-down. Who was first on the scene?"

"I think it was me and Bert Tyrell," Copps said, pointing to Tyrell, who was now sitting on a white-washed rock on the edge of the group. Tyrell, hearing his name, grinned and waved to acknowledge it.

"I'll start with you two, then." The inspector looked around the small crowd. "Who's in charge of the lodge here? Who's the boss?"

Lenny Kollberg said, "I'm the manager."

"Give us a room, will you? Somewhere I can interview people, get names and addresses."

"Use my office. Through those doors, the first room on the right."

Rowan nodded. To his sergeant, he said, "Dennis, use the firemen to seal the site off." To Copps, he said, "You can give me a hand until I get some help."

"I'm on holiday."

"Yes? Well, as soon as I know what you know, you can carry on, but right now I need you."

Copps said, "I'll get everyone in the lounge, and send them in one by one."

"Were they all here when the fire started?"

"That's my guess. The only others were me and Bert Tyrell." He pointed to the old man still sitting on the rock. "We were in a boat nearby and saw the smoke and came in. Everyone else is still out there, on the lake."

"That's convenient. Is there just one dock?"

"Effectively, yes. There's a little one along the shore, but no one from the lodge uses it."

"Who's this guy you were with?"

"Bert Tyrell. The old guy I mentioned, sitting over there. He has a shack around the point. Works part-time for the lodge."

"Reliable? Sensible? Got a full deck?"

"Oh, yeah."

"Ask him to go down to the main dock to meet people coming in, especially the picnic boat. Tell them we're investigating an incident and they must avoid the site of the fire, and stay around until we've finished talking to everyone. It shouldn't take long. First I want to find out who it is in the fire. Let's start there."

Inspector Rowan called everyone in the lounge to sit down, audience fashion, facing the front desk in the corner of the lounge. He addressed them from there. By now the news that there was a body in the fire had percolated through the crowd. Rowan began by confirming this, then asked them if anyone was aware of someone missing. He had been provided a guest list by Kollberg, and he read the names out, one by one.

One by one, the possibilities were discussed and eliminated.

No one, personally speaking, was missing anyone; no mates, no lovers, no pals, no one.

Rowan said, "We'll interrogate the rest as a group when they come ashore."

"You mean ask them the same question?" Copps said.

"Basically, yes. In this case, that is what interrogation means."

"And if you get the same answer?"

"Then we will deduce that the body doesn't belong here, won't we? Then we'll examine the body for marks of identification and evidence of any—what's that word?—trauma. Has it been subject to violent assault?"

"Isn't that kind of specialised work? Sir?"

"Yes, it is. By 'we' I meant us, the police. So as soon as they've told us what they know about who this is and how did he or she shuffle off this mortal coil, we will have done what we can. After that, they also serve who only sit and wait."

Copps recognized the type finally, someone with a taste for sarcasm in the form of prolix speech who has reached the small eminence within his profession that allows him to indulge it, a type surprising to find in the O.P.P.

There was a growing amount of chat at the back of the lounge among the group of lodge workers. One of them, Greg Eissen, the assistant chef, now put up his hand and spoke. "Chief," he said, "We are missing someone, Herbie Wengler. He hasn't been seen since breakfast. He usually spends his day off—er—getting pissed." He stayed on his feet, waiting for a response from Rowan.

Rowan said, "Herbie Wengler. Anyone else see him?"

"What does he look like?" Copps asked.

Eissen said, "He is a little old Estonian guy. He is the odd-job-man."

"Does all the shit jobs," an anonymous voice from among the workers said.

"And nobody's seen him since breakfast? Could he have gone to town?"

"He has a boat. I could check, see if it's missing."

"Check his boat, then," Rowan said. "We found some evidence that the person had been drinking. Two or three of those miniatures you get on planes."

"Any Canadian Port?"

"No."

"What kind of miniatures are they?"

"The sort you get free sometimes with a bottle of liquor."

"That's a first for Herbie. I thought he was a real wino. Still, it seems likely, don't it? Guys like Herbie will drink anything in a pinch."

Rowan asked, "When will the rest be back?"

The manager pointed through the window. "The big boat's just coming in now."

Rowan turned to Copps. "Escort them up here, would you, Sergeant? All of them, including the crew." He turned to the assembled guests and workers. "Thank you very much," he said. "Please leave now and enjoy your holiday, but stay out of this room until I've finished with it. And Mr. Manager, where does this Herbie Wengler live? Sleep, I guess?"

When the manager looked uncomprehending, the assistant chef called out. "He's got a little room of his own at the end of the bunkhouse. It's his permanently. I mean he keeps his stuff there when the camp's closed after the season's over. The other guys don't like him sleeping in the main bunkhouse."

"Why?"

"He stinks."

Rowan turned to his sergeant, "Go down with this man and seal the room, Doug. Just in case."

It was obvious to the passengers as they came off the boat that the day had turned serious. The air was full of the smell of a quenched fire; tiny bits of carbon were still being wafted from the burned-out cabin, and they had to walk past the site of the fire to reach the lodge.

Brendan Copps called out, "Would you please keep your children with you until the inspector has spoken to everyone. We'd like you to go in to the lodge. This won't take long."

In the next fifteen minutes Copps learned the meaning of "shepherding" as he watched for strays who wanted to go to their own cabins first. In the end, they were all seated, waiting for Rowan to address them.

Rowan took several sentences to reach the subject of his speech, which was that there had been a fire, and that it had caused a fatality. "We are only guessing at this point in the proceedings, but so far we have only identified, or rather, failed to identify one person. My first question, then, does anyone know of anyone else who is missing?"

The buzz stopped at Mrs. Hepburn who rose to speak. "The honeymooners," she said. "I don't know their names."

Lenny Kollberg said, "I'll give you their names. They're registered. Right now, though, they are somewhere out there in a canoe. They left after breakfast."

"Anyone see them return?"

Silence.

"Anyone else?" Rowan asked.

Deborah Wilkie had quietly joined the group, sitting at the back. Now she put up her hand. "My husband, Roger Wilkie," she said. "He went to town and he hasn't come back."

Copps whispered something in Rowan's ear. Rowan said, "Did he drive in to town?"

"No. One of the camp workers took him in his boat."

"Henry Hyacinth," Lenny Kollberg offered. "A guide."

"Has this Henry Hyacinth returned?"

"I just talked to him about Mr. Wilkie," Kollberg said. "He didn't bring him back."

"Then we can assume your husband is still in town," Rowan said. "When he comes back, I'll tick him off. Anyone else?"

"The bird-watchers," Winnie said. She explained.

"David took them out to Spinner Lake," Tyrell said. "Want me to watch for them, send them to you?"

"Yes. That would be the thing to do. All right, ladies and gentlemen. Please carry on. I don't want to keep you hanging about. The only thing I ask, those of you who have cars, please do not leave the lodge just yet. There may be more questions. If you have to go, check out with me or my sergeant."

Everyone filed out, excited by the news.

Deborah Wilkie waited. She was frightened of the route Rowan's investigation might take, whether it could lead to her and Lenny Kollberg. As she thought about it, she saw that she could not be sure that their affair was a secret. They had met too often for that. In the past, when it crossed her mind, it seemed a small risk, that someone here or in town would whisper in her husband's ear. But this time, someone who had seen her walking alone, in the vicinity, before the fire was noticed, might find it significant enough to pass on. Her affair with Kollberg would be a tasty piece of gossip, and the police investigation would be felt to be a legitimate chance to pass it on without looking like a snoop.

A lot depended on this inspector. Deborah watched and listened and decided he was a bit of a peacock, keen to display his cleverness, then decided her best hope of keeping a lid on the story would be to ask him to do just that, to flatter him into it. When the room was empty, she approached him. "I'd like a word, Inspector," she said. "To tell you about where I was this afternoon."

Rowan looked at his notes. "In your cabin, didn't you say? Reading?"

"I was in the manager's suite, Mr. Kollberg's, and we weren't reading."

Rowan organized his reaction to this. He put down his pencil, laced his fingers, and looked, slightly theatrically, out the window. "I see," he said. Soon he found words to clear his way. "Did this put you in a position to notice anything or anyone unusual?"

"The only thing unusual I noticed through the window was the smoke from the fire. I don't think anyone saw me going back to my cabin."

"Why are you telling me this? It sounds—irrelevant."

"I hope it is, but I had time to think while you were dealing with the other guests. I don't *think* anyone saw me go back to the cabin, but someone might have, and might have seen me previously go to the manager's room. I've spent time with Lenny more than once, here and in town. As I think about it now, for all I know the whole lodge is in on my secret. Someone might tell you that and you might feel the need to ask me about it and someone might overhear and that would really increase their interest. So I'm telling you now. It's not something I would want my husband to hear about."

Rowan said, "Good. Thanks. And it will help if I already know when someone tries to tell me, won't it? I can flick it off my cuff."

"Yes, you can."

"And what about Signor Kollberg?"

"Who?"

"Your partner. Does he know what you've just said?"

"I'm going to tell him now, if that's okay with you."

"The truth?"

"Oh, yes. He might try to protect me with some story, and you'd have a problem. Two different stories." She felt in charge of her own story now, doing well.

"You've done a lot of thinking about this, haven't you?"

"Something like this makes you think."

"Then I guess the great thing is that I know exactly where you both were. If you're telling me the truth, it needn't go beyond me, except into my report, of course."

"And who will see that?"

"Just my boss. Once we've identified the body—that's the important thing—well, we'll see."

Deborah stood up. "Don't screw up my life if you don't have to, Inspector."

"It sounds to me as if you are in a fair way to screwing it up yourself, but that's your business. I won't make any unnecessary inquiries."

"I'll be grateful."

"But I need to establish the veracity of what you're saying."

"The what? You mean you don't believe me?"

"You could be making this up. I don't know why."

"Nor do I, for Christ's sake. So ask him."

"Kollberg?"

"No, the Peeping Tom who was watching us through the window. Of *course* Kollberg. Lenny. Who else? And do it now, so I can forget about it."

"Can you give me something specific, something unusual he would remember? So I can corroborate what you're telling me."

Deborah took her time replying. Then she took the inspector by the elbow and drew him off to a corner to emphasize the private nature of what she was about to tell him. Slowly, steadily, sending again by the deliberateness of her response that she was telling the truth, she said, "We did it twice—you know, fornicated—that the word?" She leaned forward to whisper something more in his ear, her eyes bright with deceit, "That the sort of thing, Inspector?"

Rowan said, "There's no need for this."

"Oh, no? I thought there was. I thought that's what you wanted, something you could verify the veracity of. Lenny will confirm it all if you ask him nicely. I've seen them do that on television, police ask people separately about things, see if the stories are the same. I'll be off now, then. I'll send my husband over when he comes back." She left Rowan arranging his notes.

Two more O.P.P. vehicles appeared, a squad car and a panel truck. Two uniformed constables and a sergeant climbed out and three men in civilian clothes. "Where's Inspector Rowan?" one of the civilians asked. "That you? I'm Inspector Timpson, from the area headquarters; these are my men. And this is Doctor Taber, and this is our photographer. So fill me in. There is a body, you said. Is it suspicious?"

"We haven't been able to identify it yet, though we have one name. Man named Herbie Wengler. I've had everybody together and he's the only one who seems to be missing. If it's not him, it's an outsider, wandered into the cabin, set it on fire. An Indian, maybe."

"Why Indian?"

"From the reservation. Up at the narrows."

"Or a white man, from the town. One of those 'rubbies' who hang around the mission."

"True. We've got a few of them."

"Where is this body?"

"I'll show you."

"Just point, would you. Keep down the contamination."

The three uniformed men led the way to the mound of wet black ash that had been alive that morning. The doctor knelt for a few moments beside it. One of the civilians took a lot of pictures, then nodded to the policemen, who had unloaded a stretcher from the truck. Now, with a minimum of disturbance, they got the body wrapped and loaded on to the stretcher and into the truck. "I'll do it tonight," the doctor said.

Lenny Kollberg said, "Can we offer you a cup of coffee, Doctor?"

"You can, but what I really want is a sundowner. I was interrupted while I was doing the crossword before I had my regular one. Scotch, a large one, no water, no ice."

"We can manage that, I think. Tommy?" He signalled to the assistant manager who was waiting for something to do.

The inspector from the investigating squad turned to Rowan. "You have what you need to keep this place tight?" he asked.

"Me?"

"It's your case if it's anybody's. So far, just accidental death. But you never know. The fire guys need the site, anyway, see if they can find the cause." He turned to Kollberg. "Would there have been a fire lit, in the fireplace?"

"There might have been some embers left from yesterday. The cabin was unoccupied today."

"It doesn't take much. It's high season for fires. Ask the firemen. I'll give you a call when the medic's finished, tonight or tomorrow. Let's go, boys."

"Hang on." The doctor reached out a hand for the whiskey that the assistant manager was carrying, swallowed the drink in a gulp, winced, and handed back the glass. "You make that yourself?" he asked Kollberg, and set off towards the parked cars.

The police and the fire department men left after sealing off the area around what once was Cabin Eight with official yellow tape, both groups promising to return the next morning to conduct their investigations. The fire chief needed to make a report on the probable cause of the fire, which seemed almost certainly to have been accidental, perhaps by an ember from the hearth, or by a cigarette butt. The police needed some identification from the autopsy in order to set up their investigation.

The identity of the victim of the blaze might become clear when the doctor had conducted an autopsy, but it was generally agreed that since everyone from the lodge was accounted for, if it wasn't Herbie Wengler, it was probably a vagrant or someone from the reserve.

By the time Herbie tied his boat up and walked through the outer buildings to the lodge a gold-painted sky was waiting for the sun to finish setting. The first person to see him was Marcel, out cleaning up the leaves the little storm had left behind.

"Jesus H. Christ," Marcel said, as Herbie came close. "We thought you was dead. Where you bin? In the lake? You look like you just drowned."

"I was in town," Herbie said, beginning his new story. "I went in this morning to get a pair of gloves like yours." He held up the gloves. "I met Henry Hyacinth and we had a beer and he asked me to help him with a new stove up to his cabin on the reservation. Heavy bugger. Took all day."

"You ain't heard about the fire and the dead guy? You missed a lot of hoo-ha." Marcel put down his rake and told Herbie the story. "We all thought it might be you."

"I was in town," Herbie said. "Buying some gloves." He held them up.

. "I guess no one saw the going of you, and when they counted heads you seemed to be the one missing."

"I just went to town to buy these gloves, then I helped Henry Hyacinth with his stove."

"Right. So you said. Henry didn't say anything 'cause nobody asked, I guess. So who's the dead guy?"

"Some guy," Herbie said. "Some guy, I guess."

The probability that they would not know the dead person cheered everybody up, and dinner that night had a slightly festive air. Lenny Kollberg, who had been a bit at sea as to how he should react, now offered a drink on the house to help everyone get over "a bit of a fright."

Before they went over to the lodge for dinner, Mrs. Donner said, "Now, Paul, I want you to watch your tongue. No jokes, please, and for heaven's sake be nice to that Mrs. Hepburn."

"Was Mrs. Hepburn with anyone today?" Paul Donner asked the table, when they were all seated. "I feel a responsibility for her, having driven her away yesterday."

The mood was festive; the cabin fire had been as exciting as it was tragic, the victim being unknown.

"She was helping that girl they have with the children," Winnie said. "I watched her for a while; she did a great job. Those kids talked non-stop, but she organized games for them all the time we were on the island, and even afterwards on the boat, I watched her invent a sort of car game, identifying trees and seeing who would be the first to see the next bird. She just talked through them, never getting impatient as far as I could see. And being kids, and no one shutting them up, they just talked back, interrupting her and each other. She did the same. For the last hour she had them all playing charades, I think. They were in two teams, anyway."

"Yes, it was charades." Mrs. Hepburn had just joined them. "We limited ourselves to only the characters on children's television. It worked quite well. Of course, they were from different ages, but they are like you—us, I mean—they had all seen plenty of each other's television shows because they'd rather watch anything on television than do something creative, but this way, at least, they make something creative out of what is really passive. That is the important thing…"

"Mrs. Hepburn!" said Paul Donner authoritatively.

"You are going to say something rude, something with a swear word in it," she said. "I can tell. I always can with people like you. There was a man in a London hotel I was staying at, London, England, I mean, not…"

Donner held up his hand to stop the flow. "I'm merely going to insist that you give us a chance to tell you how much we admire you and the way you spent your day and improved ours. I shall recommend to that manager that he imburse you for one day's lodging, and he can put it on my bill if he likes. I'm rich and I can afford it, though if anyone else wants to share this with me, I will understand."

Mrs. Hepburn said, derisively, "Imburse me? What…?"

"No, no, no." Donner cut her off. "I insist. Don't say a word. No. Not a word. Don't upset me. Now Mrs. Hepburn, let's all go and watch television. I've become quite a fan of *Jeopardy*."

"I was just going to ask what 'imburse' meant. I don't think there is such a word. It's like 'gruntled'. All right, then, Mr. Moneybags. Let's go. I like *Jeopardy* too."

The door of their cabin opened and closed quietly. Simon said, "'Awake! Arise, my love and fearless be / For o'er the southern moors I have a home for thee'. We can go as soon as you've finished packing. I just need a pee."

"You paid the bill? What with? I've got our money."

"I used my new VISA card. The assistant manager is not even going to charge us for tonight."

"What about dinner?"

"That we have to pay for. It's not part of the daily package."

"No, I meant, about us getting dinner. I don't want to eat here, sitting out there, people looking at us."

"I thought of that. We'll eat in town. The assistant manager mentioned a couple of places. The Kentucky Fried Chicken sounded like the best bet."

"Did he ask why we wanted to leave?"

"Oh, sure. I said you felt self-conscious about losing your virginity."

"Me! For God's sake. Oh, I see, you're joking. I'll have to get used to that."

"He was very sympathetic. Very understanding."

"Oh, stop it. Come on, let's get out of here before he comes over to say goodbye."

They crept quietly down the hall, out of the lodge, through the trees, to the parking lot.

In the car he said, "You drive. I want to look something up." He took his bag onto his knees and rummaged to find a small black book.

"The Bible?" she asked.

"Sort of. Listen: 'And they are gone: aye, ages long ago / These lovers fled away into the storm'."

"What are you talking about? It's not raining now. Where are we staying tonight?"

"I told you. I have a home for thee."

"And something to eat, I hope. I'm starving. Are you sure that Kentucky Fried Chicken place will be open?"

The news from the autopsy the next morning simplified both inquiries. The doctor established that though the body was badly burned, the fire had probably not caused [his] death. The lungs were reported completely free of smoke, indicating he had stopped breathing before any smoke had reached him; the cause of his death was a massive heart attack, perhaps nothing to do with the fire. The police had not yet identified the body, but hoped to do that through some personal jewelry he wore.

What had started in Deborah Wilkie's mind as a possibility now blossomed into a full-scale suspicion. She even guessed what Wilkie might have been doing. She took the police inspector aside, told him what she thought, and he told his sergeant to drive her into the town to see the evidence.

It was all there, the wristwatch, the gold bracelet, the gold neck chain—she did not need to identify the body, but that was required and it was not so gruesome a task as she feared—a quick glimpse at the familiar face, blackened by smoke but untouched by the flames, was enough.

The police sergeant waited to help her, expecting her to want to get back to the lodge, but she asked him to find out if Wilkie had a solicitor, and where she could find him.

"Didn't he ever talk about one? He must have used someone a lot in the real estate business. I'll find out. Let me get you a cup of coffee while I make a few phone calls."

In no time at all he emerged from the O.P.P. office with the name and address of Wilkie's solicitor, whose own office was across the street. "When you've finished, I'll take you back to the lodge, pick up your things."

Wilkie's solicitor, the lawyer Radford, a man Deborah had never met, had more questions than answers.

Deborah cut off the routine condolences he offered. "Is there a will?" she asked.

The solicitor stared at his hands, the backs of which were covered in eczema sores. He scratched them soothingly for a few moments, then took a file from a cabinet and removed a document.

Deborah saw the words 'Last Will and Testament' on the front cover.

"I prepared this a week ago," the solicitor said.

She sat back in her chair. "Read the important bits. What did he decide to have happen?"

"He instructed me that he wished to leave everything to his brother."

"Everything?"

"The lot." He seemed to be smirking.

"Bastard." Then, "Nothing for me? Did he say why?"

"I gathered he thought you had been unfaithful."

"Gathered that, did you? Can't I deny that? I can contest it, can't I? Say he went gaga at the end? Something like that."

"That's a very conventional response, and judges are often willing to listen to it. You would need some verification, of course."

"A crooked doctor? That happens on TV a lot."

"I'm quite new here myself, but I doubt if you would find one in a town this small. Not one willing to perjure himself for a stranger. No, I meant evidence given by others of unusual behaviour."

"I could get a couple of people to swear what a bastard he was, but since he always has been and I should have known, that wouldn't be any use, would it? What about my marital rights? I've been trying to get up to speed on this stuff. There was this woman, this widow in Manitoba, who went to court and got half the property her husband had left. Isn't that standard nowadays? Look, Mr. Radford, I have nothing. Nothing. There must be something I can do."

The solicitor leaned back, smiling wide now, then bounced his chair forward and leaned on the desk. "You have grounds, all right, but there isn't any need," he said, quietly, almost whispering. "This so-called will is only a draft. It's not even signed. As far as I know, and I do know, there is no other will. He died intestate. His brother has no status. You are his rightful and legal heir."

The words failed to carry any meaning.

They looked at each other for some seconds, he smiling and smiling, she trying to make sense of what he was saying. Finally she said, "Don't play any more games, Mr. Radford. Speak English. Where do I stand? Tell me what comes after the next 'but'. You know—'except'."

"That is what I am telling you. There aren't any 'buts'. There's a brother, but he has no claim. You stand to get everything." He nodded the good news.

Now she drew the draft of the will to her, borrowed his pen, and wrote "EVERYTHING?" in big letters on the cover.

"Everything," he said. "Including the lodge." He took back his pen and made a large tick beside "Everything."

"The WHAT!" It came out as a scream. "The lodge! This isn't you being cute, is it? Are lawyers allowed to make jokes?"

The nodding slowed down and stopped. "I swear. He just finished signing the papers buying the lodge yesterday. I guess he planned to surprise you with it."

"He's done that all right." Deborah almost immediately could recreate the whole scene, Wilkie's planned "overnight stay in town," the sneaking back by car, holing up in Cabin Eight, believing that was where she had a rendezvous. Then what he had planned—divorce, cut her out of the will? Christ!

He probably really had known about her and Lenny for some time. She found she was trembling. "What happens next?"

"Legally? You hire a solicitor. You don't have to, of course, but it's usual—and I'm bound to say, wise—and instruct him to look after your affairs. I looked after your husband's affairs; everything is in order. I could hand over to your solicitor tomorrow."

She looked at him for some time, playing back in her head all that he had said in the last few minutes, thinking about how pleased he'd looked when he was talking, then said, "You didn't like Roger very much, did you?"

"I never let my feelings about a client come into it," he said. "You don't, as a solicitor."

"He thought you were a good solicitor," she said. "He called you 'the lizard'."

It was as if she had pressed the "Pause" button. He stopped collecting together the papers on his desk and looked at her, then out the window before responding, "'The lizard'. That was my name? And why was that?"

"I've no idea," she said. "He just had names for everybody." But she had, looking at the solicitor's hands. Scaly, he meant, she thought. Poor guy. The solicitor had seemed to be exuding good will until she made the thoughtless remark about Wilkie's name for him. She had not realized how unpleasant it would sound.

"Why don't we leave things as they are?" she said.

Radford was once again moving papers around his desk in a tidying-up gesture, now preparing for his next client. "Until you've had time to think, you mean? Fine. Make an appointment with our secretary when you're ready." He waved to the door to indicate where she would find the secretary. "I'll let her know to expect you." He started to get up.

"No. I mean why don't you represent me, look after me?"

He sat down to think about what she was saying. "Tidy things up for you, you mean? That won't take long; I've pretty well got everything in order. But there may be aspects of his affairs I know nothing about."

"Shady stuff, you mean?"

"He often used cash when a cheque would have been more normal."

"But not as your client, eh?"

He shook his head but said nothing.

"So, now we know, I'll ask you again. Will you look after me?"

He said. "Take some advice first, please. There is a substantial amount of money here. You could ask the manager at the bank. Get some advice. Find out if I'm the best man for the job." It was as if the blood in his veins had started flowing again. He smiled a little. "Then I'll be glad to."

This was business, she thought, the way they do it. It sounded all right to her. "In the meantime," she said, "will you look after settling up his affairs? Probate. What's probate? You hear about it. You know, start the wheels turning. You sure about the lodge?" Her brain was spinning.

"I'm quite sure about the lodge and everything else. He planned to fire the manager, Mr. Kollberg, on the spot, and take over himself."

"Why? Why fire Lenny? He's a pretty good manager."
"He gave me the impression that he suspected him of something."

"Nothing in particular, though."

"Yes: that you had been unfaithful with him. Very well, I'll act to do whatever has to be done until you give me some more orders. Nice to meet you, Mrs. Wilkie." He put a scaly hand across the desk. Deborah had read enough fiction to wonder if the disease was an outward and visible manifestation of some inner corruption, a symbol that he was crooked, but common sense very quickly took hold. She liked what he'd shown her so far, and she made a resolve to accept his suggestion, but to check his advice with the bank manager until she felt comfortable enough to rely on it herself. She liked him personally, too. They shook hands.

She said, "One thing. I don't have any money, and I can see I'll need some…"

"Ask Joe Studleigh, the bank manager, when you ask him about me. Tell him to call me. We'll look after you."

"Yes? Just like that? Then it's true. You guys are all in the same club." She smiled now. "I'll call in on him right away."

It took no time for Studleigh, the bank manager, to confirm that she was now one of his favoured clients, and arrange a line of credit. She drew out two hundred dollars right away.

First things first, she thought. As soon as it's settled I'll get myself a nice little Audi; I've always liked them. A Mini would be fun, though; I'm not too old for a Mini.

Second thoughts prevailed: Roger's car will do me for now, a nearly new Ford something-or-other, nothing flashy; he always said people wouldn't like to see him making a pisspotful of money. Later on, though, an Audi or a Mini.

As for the lodge, by the time Deborah had driven around the lake and pulled into the parking lot she knew exactly what she wanted to do. She and Wilkie had stayed here often enough as guests (now, she realized, all the while he was smoking the place out without even telling her what he was up to). She had had plenty of time to observe the running of the lodge, to notice what was wrong and, to be fair, what was right about the way the lodge was run, what ought to change. These observations now became interesting, turned into ideas. Nothing major yet. That would come, but, for instance, she had heard one or two guests who had slept late having trouble finding someone to bring them coffee in the lounge after the breakfast service was over. It wouldn't take much, she thought, to put in a permanent coffee pot on one of the side tables, and a plate of donuts— no—croissants; in the afternoon there should be tea always available. And some newspapers, not just the local paper, but

The Globe and *The Toronto Star*, she'd often heard one of the older guests, made glum by the internet, asking at the desk for a real newspaper. She'd actually suggested the idea to Lenny Kollberg but he never bothered. "These people," he had said, "come here for a holiday. They want to get away from the day-to-day news."

Then why are they looking for newspapers, she had wondered to herself, but it wasn't worth arguing about then. Now there wouldn't be any argument, would there?

The news had preceded her, always the way in a small community. Lenny Kollberg was waiting for her in the lodge, sitting in one of the armchairs in the lounge. She walked by him as he stood up to intercept her. "Let's talk in your office," she said.

"I'm sorry about Roger," he said, when he closed the door. He stood waiting for her to speak: their relationship might have changed. She was the boss; he was the manager of her lodge.

"Take a seat, Lenny," she said. "You know better than that. Apparently he was already dead when the fire reached him, so he didn't suffer. And you know better than anybody that he and I were non-starters, but I'll keep up appearances. I think I'll stay home for a few days, for the sake of those appearances. He just had one brother, so it won't be a big funeral, although in a small town a lot of locals might come. So be it. I'll get that wedding caterer in town to arrange some sandwiches. And some drinks. Now, let's say I'll come back in on Monday next week. Give me one of the double cabins. Do we have a full house then?"

"I don't think so."

"Make sure, though. Ask Tommy. I won't eat with you and the other management staff at first. I'll eat in the dining room with the guests. That way I'll hear all the gossip."

"And us?"

"Us?" Then a slow dawning, that she had been making assumptions that they were in the same space, but they weren't, quite. "Us, you mean. You and me? We've had that conversation, Lenny."

"Doesn't this change things?"

"I need time to think, Lenny, my love. As you say, this changes things for me, but not with us, I think. I'll need you here for the foreseeable future."

Lenny said, not looking at her, "You may not need me here that long. Maybe I should pack up and leave tonight?"

"Why? Lenny, all I'm saying is that I am going to be hands-on. That's all. Okay?"

"And me? How long for?"

She leaned back in her chair. "I have to tell you, Lenny, Roger planned to fire you on Friday. On the spot."

"So maybe I should quit now."

"I hope you won't. The lodge would be hard to run without you. And I need you, Lenny. Not for the lodge; for myself." After a pause she said, "Now that it's possible, I think I want to live with you. As soon as it's decent. What say you?"

He was silent as she watched him respond wordlessly. "Good," she said and changed the subject. "So, you did the hiring of the rest of the management staff and none of them got renewable contracts. Right? I just want to get things straight in my head before I talk to them."

"We had to give Sammy, the chef, an understanding, but there's nothing on paper. Nobody else has anything. That's normal. They're all seasonal workers."

"I'll speak to Sammy; he's a pretty good cook. Okay, Lenny, so in public it's Mr. Kollberg, the manager, and Mrs. Wilkie, the owner, as always. Look after the lodge, and me, Lenny, and I'll look after you. I need you, not just to run this place, but, well, to be with me. That's all I can say. My head is full of stuff; I'll sort it out. Bit by bit. Does Tommy know?"

"About us?"

"Us? No, for God's sake. About Roger, my husband."

"Word has got around."

"Find Tommy, will you, and send him to see me. I'll use your office for an hour or two, then I'll go back to town." It was her first order. She turned to rummage in her bag.

At the door, he said, "It would help me if you told the staff what is happening."

"I'll do better than that, Lenny. I'll tell them I have complete confidence in you and them and your ability to carry on and run things as they've always been run. That no one should notice any difference. And then I'll disappear, too upset to stay around, until Sunday week, say, maybe longer until it's clear that you are still in charge. That'll show them that I have complete confidence, won't it? One more thing: you tell them how important it is there be no gossip, no speculation, that if you hear anyone talking to the guests, or even among themselves about the tragedy or me, you'll let them go. They'll do it anyway, of course, but warning them will keep it down. Now find Tommy."

"Mrs. Wilkie?"

"Come in, Tommy. Sit down. I'm trying to get a fix on the management staff. You like it here? Working here, I mean."

It was crude, clumsy, but she had to start somewhere and she didn't want to go into a verbal mating dance to lead up to telling him that she liked the look of him, approved of the way he did his job and would welcome any suggestions he had to make about the running of the lodge.

He said, after a pause that showed that he hadn't considered the question before, "It's a good summer job. And Mr. Kollberg is easy to work with."

"That's it?"

"That's a lot, these days, for a student, Mrs. Wilkie."

"When are you leaving?"

"September 15th, ma'am."

"Can you stay until the 30th? Help close the lodge down?" She probably didn't need him for that, but she might next season and it was all she could think of at the moment by way of showing him she approved of him without going too far.

"I'd have to go in to Toronto for an overnight, to get myself registered in the Hotel Management Program at the university for next year."

"And find a place to live?"

"That's already arranged."

"It would be worth a bonus of two weeks' pay. A month's pay for an extra two weeks work. You could fly from Winnipeg to Toronto, and stay overnight. I'll pay the fare, and a hotel."

"I'll find a way, then."

"Good. Now about the lodge. When I come back on Monday week, I want a list from you of all the things you would change if you were in my position."

"I can't do a study of the place. That's the job of an outsider."

"Nor do I want that. I just want to know what you would do to run the place better. For instance, a little thing: I think there should be coffee always available in the lounge for anyone who misses breakfast, and tea in the afternoon. I think we should turn that bloody music off in the lounge, or down, at least. That's a big thing. Your turn."

Li had been looking worried. His face cleared. "And we should supply clothes—not uniforms, maybe just polo shirts—to all the staff so the guests know who to ask for things," he suggested.

"Including you?"

"Everybody except maybe Mr. Kollberg."

She laughed. "Why not him? Doesn't he like dressing up?"

"He likes to look the part. In a polo shirt he would look like the wrong kind of manager."

She let that go. "And you?"

"I'd be okay with a polo shirt, but I'd have a badge, too. Maybe we should have shirts and badges all round."

"So will you want to be coming back next year?"

"I'd like to."

The conversation had gone far enough. She said, "I don't know what comes next, Tommy. I have to think. Make me a list of all the other things you would do if you were me. Who else do you think I should talk to today?"

He had to ask. "Is Mr. Kollberg in on this?"

"Of course. I've already talked to him, made clear what our options are. What I'm doing is setting up a kind of instant 'Suggestions' box, one the staff can put their ideas in, starting with you. And I'll leave the box set up. But you make a good point. I'm jumping the gun a little. I don't want to go behind anyone's back, but I do want all the ideas I can get from the staff about how to improve things. It was Mr. Kollberg's idea that I should talk to you. He's the manager."

"Okay, then. The only one we couldn't do without, including me, is Sammy, the chef. Talk to him."

"I've already asked to see him." She stood up. With Sammy, Lenny Kollberg, and Tommy Li signed up she felt sure already they could open next season and scratch any talk of a casino. "I'll be back in ten days," she said.

"What happened to the old biddy from Winnipeg?" Copps asked. "I thought you were stuck with her."

"She doesn't need me like that. Just as someone to tell her story to."

"And now she's told it? Okay. Now, what about us? I've been thinking."

Winnie said, "Once upon a time I had a boyfriend who had been in training to be a priest. Then one day, he said to the man in charge of whatever they call a group of apprentice priests that he'd been thinking. Afterwards, when he was leaving the order, the chief priest told him that within the order, the phrase, 'I've been thinking' always meant 'I have doubts, big ones'. What have you been thinking?"

"I'll tell you, but don't interrupt, okay? I decided to tell you exactly what's going on in my head. Then you can tell me about what's in yours."

"I'll see about that. I don't think I'm quite there, yet. Tell me how I fit into the roster of women you've known. Is that what you mean by thinking?"

"That's the start of it. But there's more."

"You mean I'm going to hear about the one who has just turned up on the dock with the son you never knew you had?"

"Nothing like that. No secrets. I don't have any secrets. Do you?"

"Nothing that would matter to you. I was engaged once, did I tell you?"

"You never told me what happened, who broke it off."

"He did. He wrote me one of those 'Dear John' letters. 'Dear Winnie' in his case. We graduated from veterinary college together, and the wedding was supposed to be the next event. We'd been planning it the whole last semester."

"Were you—what's the term?—laid out by it? By grief, I mean."

"It was sort of a relief. I didn't tell anyone for a day or so, until I was used to the idea, giving me time to realize that, compatible as we were—everyone saw us as the ideal couple with matching interests—his were dairy cattle—I had finally realized what love is because I wasn't distraught because I didn't love him. A lot of people get married and manage very well without love, I found out later, but I didn't want to then. I was still too young. But, hey, this is your story. So tell me."

They were side by side, lightly pressed together in the big bed that Dempsey's provided for married couples (you specified on the registration form whether you wanted two singles or a double), his arm under her head. The events of the day had taken away some of their energy but not all. As if they had talked about it, they had coupled gently, pleasurably, their bodies talking to each other, joining each other when they were both ready. Now they talked.

Copps said, "I was planning to tell you about everything that has happened to me, how I feel about us, about the future, but now I don't want to."

She laughed. "What do you want to talk about?"

"Us, of course. One of us has got to come clean, go naked. Okay, so I will. I don't believe it has ever happened to me before, but I'm sure it has now. I love you and I want to marry you. There." He looked around in the mock-comic gesture of a man who is afraid of being overheard.

Nothing much happened for a long time. She wiggled her feet to smooth out the sheet that had got caught between her ankles. He took back his arm and laced his fingers together over his belly.

She said, "There are problems."

"I know. What about the work? Where we will live."

"Don't cut me off. That's Rule no. 1. I want to make a small speech. Just a couple of sentences. Like this: I've been thinking of all the things we have to sort out before we get married. First, I have a good practice in Newbury; you're just stationed there. What happens if they transfer you? Do I give up Newbury and go with you? Or do you come back for weekends, if they let you? See I've been going round and round on this and other things we have to settle in order to get married."

"I make that ten."

"Ten what?"

"Sentences."

"And I haven't finished yet. I found the answer."

"Which is?"

"We'll never get it sorted before we get married, so let's get married first, then sort it all out later."

He laughed and took her hand and placed it over his heart and put his hand on top of hers. "I've been doing the same thing about my job. Thinking. I've been wanting to quit, but I thought I shouldn't resign until I had something else in place. Then I thought maybe I should just quit and see what happens. Find some way to go back to farming. So here goes." He sat up without dislodging their hands. "What I'll do, I'll stay in the force until they try to transfer me. Then I'll quit, but by then I will have something else lined up. Right?" He lay back, finished.

"It'll do." She took back her hand, scratching his belly lightly on the way. "Now go to sleep. Tomorrow we can play 'Happy Families', and you can tell me about this farming idea. Farming? God!"

To Franny, Tommy said, "She wants me to stay until September 30th. And she asked me about next year."

"What about us? Are we moving in together? In Toronto?"

"I'd like to. My parents won't like it, but I'm tired of the frat house life."

"Why won't your parents like it? Immoral?"

"Oh no, nothing Like that. It's just that—well, they're old country Chinese. They're not too crazy about having white foreign devils in the family."

"We're not there yet, tell them, just keeping house together to cut down on expenses."

"And Dennis. What about him?"

"I'll be in Toronto first. It will give me time to tell Dennis."

"That won't be any fun, will it?"

"We were practically engaged."

"Maybe he's met someone else, too. The girl who makes toast at the Banff Springs Hotel, maybe."

"I wish. I don't feel very good about it. I think I was his first real girlfriend."

"Not his last, though. What about your stuff in Toronto? Mrs. Wilkie's giving me a weekend in Toronto to do what I need to organize for the semester. I can use part of it to get together anything you want brought over to the apartment."

"I think I'll give all the house stuff, the sheets and kitchen things, to Molly to kind of compensate her for having to find a roommate at the last minute."

"When will you meet Dennis?"

"I'll go out to the airport when his plane comes in."

"Right. A girl I knew last year told me about a time like this when she went out to the airport to meet her boyfriend after a summer apart. Your kind of situation. She said as soon as he kissed her she knew it was over. Your guy will know, too, right away, as soon as you kiss him. Meet him at ARRIVALS, take him into the airport bar, tell him you have something to say, make him sit down and kiss him. It's the only way."

Acknowledgments

The author would like to thank *Descant Magazine*, which previously published an excerpt of this novella.

OTHER QUATTRO FICTION